THE TIDE THAT BINDS US

ALEXIS C. MANESS

Dedication

To all of us who have ever felt *othered*, I hope you learn to embrace what is unique about you.
I can assure you there are plenty of others who are in awe of the magic within you

The Tide That Binds Us

Having a mermaid princess mysteriously murdered on her shores isn't how Queen Celestia envisioned her reign. With doubts about her worthiness to rule rising in her kingdom and outside her borders, she must prove herself capable as a young queen.

However, eliminating the threat to her people proves more difficult than she'd anticipated—especially when the enchanting mermaid, Aura, is thrust into her life, stirring up feelings and complicating the path to peace.

Will she be able to save her people and her crown? Or will she fail her first true test as queen?

Get swept into the romance, betrayal, and magic of Cessadia in The Tide That Binds Us.

Trigger Warnings

Please note that this book contains:
Branding, brief imprisonment, dead bodies, death of
Mother during childbirth (referenced), kidnapping, mild
gore, mild violence, murder, parental death (referenced),
poisoning, prejudice toward mythical creatures.

Chapter One

The wailing of the merpeople wrenched Celestia from her peaceful slumber. Something was wrong.

Their cries carried on the wind, burrowing their way into her mind so she couldn't ignore the call. She had no choice but to investigate.

She quickly wrapped an ivory, silk robe around her as she ran down the spiral staircase, the ominous glow of the moonlight chasing her as it reflected off the floors inlaid with mother of pearl. When she bounded down the castle's front steps, her toes met cool sand, which kicked up against her ankles as she closed in on the shallows where the merpeople mourned. The midnight mist wrapped thickly around her, casting a haze over everything more than a few feet in front of her.

Even still, she knew there were dozens of mermaids wading beyond shore, their tell-tale, bioluminescent glow making their presence known.

She came within speaking distance and slammed to a halt when she saw it. Saw her. It was her cousin, Princess Estrellia, the merqueen's eldest daughter.

Lying in a bed of seaweed, she looked ethereal; her long silver hair was bathed in moonlight and her iridescent skin glimmered. Before, she had blended in against the white sand, but the golden-orange scales of her tail broke through the pressing mist and darkness. As Celestia approached her, there was no ignoring the gaping hole in her chest, its jagged edges a gruesome contrast to her beauty.

One of their own was dead. Murdered.

Now she recognized the scent that stifled her breaths more than the biting cold; it was the stench of death, of a life taken brutally on her own shore.

Regaining movement in her frozen joints, she continued until the waves licked up her legs and she sank to her knees, joining her people in their cries from the edge of the enchanted, pink-and-green water that glowed brightly with magic.

Tonight, she would mourn. Tomorrow, she would be as a queen should be: composed and ready for action.

The long night of grieving bled into the early morning hours, the somber air remaining heavy even as the sun's light started to disperse the dark cloak of night. Gradually, the merpeople began to make their way back to the depths of the ocean, leaving only royalty and those who directly served them remaining.

The humans had yet to wake, but she had no doubt her council would come straight here in search of her when they found her bed empty with the covers thrown back.

Until then, they would wait in silence. The merqueen's rage hung heavy in the air. Celestia dared not speak until spoken to. While this was technically her kingdom's jurisdiction—it was clearly the doing of humans—this was an especially delicate matter.

One of the merqueen's daughters had been slain like an animal, her heart taken and her mutilated body left for all to see.

A line had been drawn. A message had been sent. And it was going to wreak havoc on their very fragile peace.

While they waited for her council to arrive, Celestia took the opportunity to gaze upon her cousin. This was, admittedly, the closest she had ever been to her, what with Estrellia being confined to the sea and she to the land.

It was odd that this was the first time she had felt a real connection to her, but they had never been close. Her relatives—who were all born of the water—thought they were superior to her. To them, she was a bastardized version of their people's legacy, born for the sole purpose of uniting the kingdoms of land and sea. She couldn't necessarily blame them. Her mother had been forced into the arrangement. The merking of the past had put political gain above his own daughter's safety.

But that also wasn't Celestia's fault. And neither was the fact that her mother died in childbirth. Nonetheless, they seemed to hold a grudge. And with her father gone, all of that anger and pain rested on Celestia's shoulders.

It was just a shame that what so many had sacrificed to unite them had only created a deeper division over time. And now, here they were, their carefully constructed truce on the precipice of collapse.

Before she could spiral further into the political nightmare that had been set in motion with the slaying of the merprincess the night before, her council strode forward, led by Tolero. Her head of council appeared stone-faced, ready to attack whatever had taken his queen from her bed. It would have been touching if she knew it wasn't just for show; he felt nothing but disdain for Celestia, disappointed the crown had passed to her.

"Your Highness." Tolero bowed stiffly. "I was so worried, I thought harm might have befallen you." He didn't even bother to infuse concern into his tone.

Her throat constricted, not quite ready to admit the truth of why they were all on that beach.

Her legs itched beneath the dry sand that had caked on overnight. Her head began to pound from the tears she had shed for these people who loathed her, and her muscles were weary from resisting the current for hours on end.

But she was a queen, and she would not shirk her duties. Especially when she still had so much to prove.

"No, I'm fine. But there's been a murder." She lifted a long finger in the direction of Estrellia's body. The other council members behind her gasped.

"Who did this?" Tolero demanded.

"We don't know who, per se. Only that it must have been a human since she was killed outside of their waters. It would appear her heart is missing, judging by the wound in her chest, but I didn't inspect further. I was waiting for you."

"Very well. Let me have a look." Tolero moved swiftly past her, his navy cloak billowing in the wind. He pulled on gloves as he bent down to inspect the body.

The waves crashed and sloshed violently against the shoreline and rocks as her aunt, the merqueen, struggled to control her anger at the scene unfolding in front of her. Celestia was sure there was nothing Meridia detested more than the thought of a human man, especially Tolero, touching her daughter's slain body.

As if on cue, she finally spoke to Celestia. "I want her back when you're finished. She doesn't belong here." Her voice was deep with threat, promising trouble if they dared deny her.

Of course, Tolero wasn't going to give in so easily, even if she was mourning the loss of one of her favorite daughters. "I think we should keep her for a day for further—"

"No. Take your time with her now, then she will be returned to the sea." Celestia infused her voice with the authority her father had taught her to use at a young age.

He would have been proud, had he been here. Although Meridia surely would have struck him down with a tidal wave at first sight.

Celestia sighed at the complexity of her role in this world, letting the weight of it burrow into her bones as she forced her feet forward to join Tolero.

He and two other councilors were inspecting a substance on their gloved fingers when she approached.

"What is it?"

"We believe it to be a poison. Specifically, a toxin designed to paralyze the body when introduced to the bloodstream—a strong one, if it was able to overpower such a creature. It would make sense. That would be the only way to draw one of them out of the water and render them powerless enough to slay. Our best guess is that they waited for her to come close enough to shore, then shot her with a poisoned arrow." Not a hint of emotion was present in Tolero's voice when discussing how the princess was incapacitated. It sent a chill through Celestia as she let her eyes roam over her cousin's limp form.

The way her silver hair tangled around her arms and the sand clung to her face made her stomach churn. Estrellia was known for being undeniably beautiful and just as vain, spending much of her time in the coves, flirting with humans from afar and lavishing in their gifts. She would have been mortified to be seen in such a state.

Celestia bent down to move the hair and sand away in an effort to restore some of her dignity, but her aunt called out.

"Do. Not. Touch. Her." The words were guttural. "If you had been doing your job as queen, this wouldn't have happened."

The words picked at a wound of inadequacy that Celestia thought she had been doing a good job mending.

"You don't tell me what to do with those who are on my land. You may reign over the sea by our treaty, but this is my territory to command, and you will treat me with the respect I'm owed." Their eyes locked as a battle of wills ensued. "I have caused no harm to you or yours. I'll do everything in my power to protect them. This was a blatant attack on our people, and the party responsible will pay. But, in order for that to happen, we must collect evidence."

Celestia stared her aunt down another moment, before turning back to the body. This time, she did not make any move to get near her.

An hour later, Tolero and his assistant had collected evidence from her body and the surrounding area, and the guards had moved her body back to the shallows for the merpeople to collect. Once her duty was done, Celestia left without another glance back at the gruesome scene that reminded her of just how much work she had to do to repair the relationship between the people of the sea and of the land.

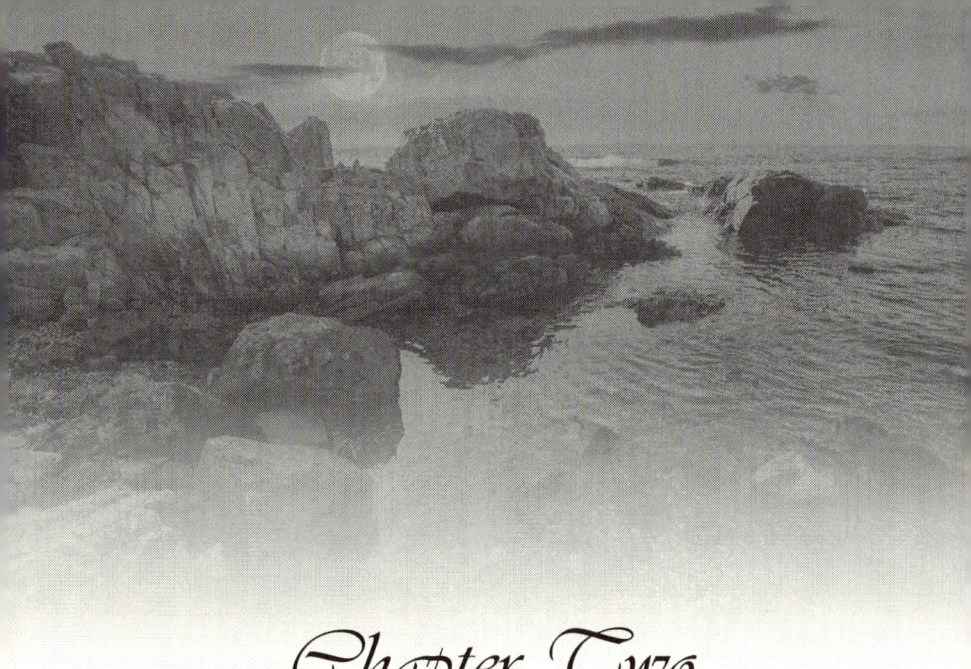

Chapter Two

*T*olero strolled into the council meeting the next morning with an air of triumph driving him forward. His notes were held firmly in his hand as he flourished them about. "As I suspected, the poisoner isn't likely to be one of our own citizens. It's made using a plant that can only be found in the northeast region of the continent."

Celestia shifted on her throne, the hard seat pressing uncomfortably to her backside. She rolled her shoulders back as she realized what he was insinuating. "You're saying it came from Mesantia?"

He nodded firmly.

"Then please tell me how that makes this situation any better?"

"It's not our people who are the threat, so it alleviates our obligation to the merpeople. We can shift our focus back to other priorities that are actually *our* problem."

"All of my people are my responsibility. Just because one of our citizens isn't to blame doesn't mean it's not our duty to resolve it."

Tolero opened his mouth to speak, but she silenced him with one hand.

"If anything, this is an even bigger problem than we previously suspected. If Mesantian citizens are emboldened enough to come here and commit such a crime, it means that we now have reason to be wary of them."

"I'm sure a letter to the king detailing the offense will prompt him to take action. I can even write it for you. The Maksim you remember from childhood is not who we're dealing with now. Ascending to the throne at such a young age has changed him. I have more experience with *King* Maksim. I know how to appeal to his senses. It'll be sorted in no time; no need for you to worry about it."

"I'm sure you do. However, I will be worrying about it and won't just be sending a letter. A princess has been slain. In doing so, they've challenged us in the most direct way possible. I can't let this go until I'm certain there will be justice."

Reedus—the council member who oversaw local affairs—stepped forward this time, interrupting their back and forth. "If I may, your majesty, I think that Tolero may be right. Maksim isn't one to take kindly to being approached aggressively, especially not by a woman. He may only be a few years older than you, but he's not what you'd call progressive. He very much follows the old ways." He had the grace to duck his head at the last part, knowing she'd take offense.

She had to appreciate the candor, but it still sparked anger she didn't know was so close to the surface.

Her voice came out gritty and tense. "I don't give a damn what Maksim does or doesn't like. If he has a problem with women in authority, he'll have to learn to deal with it, as I'm not going anywhere anytime soon. And, unfortunately for him, as rulers of neighboring kingdoms, we'll have to resolve issues together from time to time."

A third member of her council, Alexie—overseer of taxation and another relic from her father's reign—had a comment to make, as well. Of course, he sided with Reedus and Tolero. This was the way of things now. The remaining members of her father's council and those she had appointed herself were always at odds with one another. They were stuck in their old ways and struggling to find their footing in a kingdom now ruled by a woman—and a relatively young one at that—while her appointees were fighting for change and a new era between humans and merpeople. As such, these meetings almost always devolved into bickering and ended in a stalemate.

A pulsing ache was building behind Celestia's eyes as she listened to her council argue about the incident. Some wanted to ignore it, to find some way to appease the merpeople without provoking further conflict within the realm. Fortunately, there were others on her council with much more sense.

"Impossible. Meridia would send us all to early graves at the bottom of the ocean floor. And even so, they need to held accountable. They're provoking us. If we let them get away with this, they'll think us weak. Celestia is still fairly new to her throne, so ignoring this could lead to questions about her ability to lead and protect her people. That makes us vulnerable." Leani, head of her guard, had always been the most strategic and level-headed of the group. They made eye contact, Leani empathizing with her frustration at the men still refusing to listen to reason.

Five minutes later and Celestia was gripping the edge of her throne so hard that she feared her nails would snap off. When Tolero had raised his voice once again, trying to domineer the others, she'd had enough. She stood abruptly, ensuring that her bracelets scraped across the rough, shell-encrusted edges of the arms to disrupt them. With her growing frustration, her skin began to glow with the bioluminescent sheen of the power she'd inherited from her ancestors.

"We'll go to Mesantia and ask the king to hold his people accountable. I will have justice for what's happened to one of my own."

Tolero threw his hands up, contesting her idea.

Celestia pinned each of them with her gaze, her large, rounded eyes taking on the moony glow that seemed to unsettle everyone in the room. "This is not up for debate. I am the queen. What I say goes. I value your input, but your suggestion isn't one that serves the best interests of the kingdom. Understood?"

She'd need to get moving immediately to have everything in order for the morning.

"You're dismissed. Leani, walk with me please."

Each councilor bowed their head before they turned and exited the throne room in silence. When all but Leani were gone, Celestia finally descended the steps and let out a sigh that exhaled all her frustration.

Leani laughed, giving her forearm a supportive squeeze. Not only was she her most trusted advisor and the head of her guard, but, with the loss of her mother and then her father, she had also become somewhat of a parental figure to her, going out of her way to look after Celestia and helping her navigate life as queen. She'd been a close friend of her father's since they were children, so there was no doubt she could be trusted. She wouldn't be who she was today without her.

"Do you think Maksim will be diplomatic?"

Cynicism deepened the creases at the edge of Leani's amber-brown eyes. "I fear that he won't make this easy for us. If I know him, he'll be reluctant to admit one of his own are responsible, let alone punish them. You know as well as I do, he's not the most empathetic of men." Her hand rubbed the back of her neck with worry.

"I feared as much. That's why I'm going with you to Mesantia. He needs to know that we won't take no for an answer."

"Are you sure that's wise with the state of things? We wouldn't want anyone to take advantage of your absence."

"Unfortunately, I don't think there's any other option if we want to resolve this matter as diplomatically as possible." Celestia twisted a long strand of dark seafoam green hair, deep in thought as they walked past the crowds milling about in the lower level of the castle.

"Go sleep. These problems will still be here to solve when you wake. We leave at dawn."

Celestia nodded. "Can you please arrange for extra guards at the border? And we'll need a watch on the beach. Make sure they're your most trusted people. I want those who are assigned with this task to protect Meridia and the other mermaids, not provoke them in their time of mourning."

Leani squeezed her hand in reassurance before swiftly making her way out of the castle.

Each step of the walk back to her quarters on the third floor sent an ache through her body. She yearned for her bed and a quiet mind.

However, she had one last matter to deal with.

Celestia stopped by Allora's quarters on the way, asking for her assistance in readying things for tomorrow. She handled all of Celestia's personal affairs, and, thankfully, she was very efficient at her job. She needed to have her trident sharpened, suitable riding and court garments packed, and the horses readied first thing in the morning.

As soon as she crossed the threshold of her bedroom, she rushed to her bed, tossing aside the large pillows with reckless abandon. When Celestia finally pulled back the covers, she stripped out of her violet dress, leaving it in a poufy heap, and crawled into bed.

She eased into a deep sleep. Unfortunately, it was plagued by worries of their travels to Mesantia and ominous memories of the night before.

Chapter Three

After a nightmare-addled night, the next morning came far too soon. The sun had just begun to break through the clouds, casting a molten orange hue across the sky as they mounted their horses and exited the gates into the unclaimed land between the territories.

Celestia allowed herself one look back at her realm. The tall golden gates and shell-infused walls ran as far as the eye could see, but her heart still squeezed at the thought of leaving it somewhat vulnerable for the next few days. As the worry grew in the pit of her stomach, so did her resolve to get justice.

The muscles in her legs and lower back began to scream after several hours of riding, but, every time her frustration mounted, she reminded herself why she was doing this.

Noticing her discomfort, Leani urged her own horse forward until they were at an even pace.

"Riding is the worst part of travel." She tossed her a flask of water. "But the heat and dehydration will leave you just as worn down if you're not careful."

Celestia grunted. The sun beating down on her was also making her irritable. She didn't spend nearly as much time traveling as Leani and Tolero did, and she didn't think she ever could. It was only a little over a day's ride to Maksim's palace but for her it might as well have been an eternity. It didn't help that she'd inherited the unearthly pallor of her mother. Her pale skin reddened and blistered while Tolero and Leani's warm, brown complexions glowed golden under the sun's rays. Still, they all applied cream to their skin throughout the day to protect themselves—Leani insisted on it.

She tried to distract herself from her discomfort with conversation. "I haven't seen Maksim since I was barely a teen. Do you think he'll recognize me?"

Leani laughed. "Your majesty, I think you forget just how unique you are."

She shifted on her horse, uncomfortable at the mention of how much she stood out due to her unique combination of her parents' features.

While she resembled her father and had classic Cessadian features—large eyes, strong brow, prominent nose, and a wide face—she still stood out. The iridescent sheen of her mother's people caused her skin to shimmer in the sunlight and glow in the moonlight, making her a beacon for stares and curiosity. Not only that, but she also wasn't a small person, built quite a few sizes wider than the average Cessadian woman. Her figure was her mother's.

As they rode, a memory of the ball she had attended with Maksim drifted into her mind, taking her back to when their fathers first had hopes of arranging a marriage for them, despite their slight age difference. The barren landscape around them disappeared and she was transported into the grand ballroom back home.

She had walked into that ball with a genuine smile beaming across her face, her azure, silk dress perfectly tailored to hug her heavy-set figure and trailing elegantly behind her. It was one of the first times she truly felt like a beautiful princess like the ones in her fairytales.

That was until she realized most of their guests weren't staring because they were in awe of the stunning work of the royal seamstress; they were gawking at her peculiar appearance. No matter how human she was, it was never enough to blend in. Her long, seafoam-green hair, the glow of her skin and eyes, and the shiny scales along her upper arms had always made her distinctly "other." While her own people had accepted her mermaidesque appearance, those who visited from other kingdoms couldn't seem to help themselves.

After several remarks from other hopefuls vying for Maksim's attention, and smug looks from the other young men in attendance, he had simply left her to fend for herself for the remainder of the evening. She'd sat on the outskirts of the action with no one to ask her to dance or tell her she was beautiful. After years of friendship and flirting at their fathers' encouragement, he had abandoned her at the first conflict of her otherness.

She felt the deep loneliness of that night settling heavily into her as she recalled the tears she had spilled and the thick skin she'd forced herself to develop since.

Leani's soft fingers under her chin brought her back to the present. "Don't let his cruelty get to you." She stroked away a tear that Celestia hadn't registered was there. "He was never worthy of you, and he'll see that in the woman, *the queen*, you have become. We're here to assert your authority and ensure your people get justice. Don't let him get an advantage before negotiations have even begun."

Celestia nodded, but she couldn't help the brief feeling of regret that she hadn't worn a shirt with longer sleeves to cover the small patch of scales on each arm. They'd always been the hardest to conceal. Her thighs could be easily covered by flowing gowns and riding pants.

The rest of the journey to their accommodations for the night was mostly silent as they all tried to stave off the misery of the escalating heat and drying air.

Tolero kept ahead of the group, only occasionally chiming in to impart a piece of wisdom he thought Celestia would find useful when dealing with Maksim. Namely, that she should speak to him as little as possible.

By the time they made it to the home they would be staying in for the night, her nerves were frayed, and she was just as tired physically. Once they had eaten and thanked their hosts, they all retired immediately to their rooms to prepare for the even more difficult day that lay ahead of them tomorrow: trekking up the small mountain.

A jolt went through her chest, disorienting her as everything around her went hazy. Cold hands grabbed at her exposed skin and pressed firmly over her mouth. Her thoughts ricocheted frantically around her mind, unable to maintain any sense of direction. Her limbs grew increasingly foreign, going limp despite her protests. Her lips wouldn't move. She could only watch in horror and silence as the men pulled her body along, the abrasive sand searing against her exposed skin. She tried to defend herself, to call out. She couldn't do anything, even as she saw one of the men pull a long dagger from beneath his cloak. Before she had enough time to process what she was seeing, the cold metal found its way into her chest.

The shock surged through her body as she lunged forward in bed. She clutched her hands to her heart as she took in her surroundings. She wasn't on the beach. She was safe in a bed. It was only a dream; the same one she'd had last night.

She wasn't sure if it was the guilt for allowing something to happen to her cousin or the anxiety that someone would come for her next. Celestia couldn't shake the fear that had made itself at home within her since the moment she heard the shrill cries of grief calling out to her in the night.

Despite sinking back into the plush bedding and pulling the soft linen over her eyes, Celestia couldn't find sleep again. Instead, she stared through the window as her mind churned sluggishly. Eventually, the sun's rays greeted her in their full glory.

Another early morning had Celestia disgruntled from too many nights of too little sleep. It took everything in her to find the energy to mount her horse. As she swung her leg over her horse's back, she groaned in pain. She wasn't looking forward to spending any more time out in the elements, especially when her body would fight the rising altitude every inch of the way. Then there was the dread of seeing Maksim after all these years.

Each mile they drew closer to Mesantia increased her struggle to reign in the anxiety that stirred in her veins.

When they reached the iron gate built into the surrounding rock formations that marked the entrance of Maksim's palace, she fought the urge to empty the contents of her stomach. Instead, she rolled her shoulders back, inclined her chin, and set her jaw. This was her first diplomatic engagement as Queen and she'd make the right impression, no matter how much of a façade it was.

They were escorted by the Mesantian guard into the palace. She gawked at the castle walls that had been built within the mountain. She couldn't imagine how difficult it had been to establish a palace within such a space, but they made the most of the natural structure, carving out caves and tunnels. After several minutes of walking through echoing halls, they approached the throne room where Maksim waited, sitting high above them on an imposing large stone seat that was adorned with onyx and surrounded by stalagmites.

Tolero made to introduce her, but the king waved him off. "Celestia," he purred with a nod of his golden head. His deep voice reverberated around the rocky walls.

"Maksim." She tried to quell the flutter in her stomach. He was more handsome than she remembered. He'd filled out into an impressively rugged build, and it seemed his ice blue eyes had somehow become brighter, but she wouldn't let herself forget his dismissal of her all those years ago.

They stared at each other for a moment, the rest of her party shifting on their feet with anticipation.

"I wasn't expecting you, but I can't say it's an unpleasant surprise. To what do I owe the pleasure of your company? It's been, what... ten years?"

"Twelve."

"And I see not much has changed, you're just as serious as ever."

"I take my duty seriously. Which brings me to why we've come. There was a murder on our beach. Someone, one of your people it would seem, entered my kingdom in the dead of night and murdered the mermaid princess."

Maksim tsked at her. "This isn't the way things are done, Celestia. Don't you know it's rude to bring up politics before dinner?" He arched a golden brow down at her. "I know you still have much to learn so I won't take offense."

Tolero interjected before she could respond. "Our apologies, Your Majesty, this is Celestia's first time traveling to another kingdom without her father. As you said, she's still learning."

Anger flared within her, and she knew Tolero took note of the glow that had overtaken her eyes as his own gaze widened slightly. She restrained herself from looking upon Maksim until she could pull it back below the surface.

"Fine. Dinner. Then we handle what we came here for."

Maksim laughed but rose from his throne. "My servants will show you to your rooms so you can freshen up before we dine. They'll retrieve you in an hour to escort you, it's easy to get lost here."

Celestia quickly changed into court-appropriate attire, hoping to catch Tolero and remind him of their precarious position before he humiliated her further. She fumed as she clasped her cloak in place.

When she looked in the mirror, she was pleased with what she saw. The sharp shoulders of her midnight blue cape paired with the metallic breastplate she wore over her grey dress presented an imposing figure, even if she was nervous about what the night would hold. She ran her fingers over the shell-shaped silver cups that guarded her chest, down the soft grey fabric of her skirts, and over the flowing sleeves that cinched at her wrists—keeping them in place and preventing anyone from seeing the scales that graced her arms—and gave herself one final nod of approval.

She especially loved the sounds of her skirt swishing angrily against the polished, onyx floor as she walked briskly to Tolero's quarters, allowing it to announce her imminent arrival.

Chapter Four

*M*aksim had enough respect for her to place her at the foot of the table, although she found it quite discomforting to stare him down as the rest of their party made idle conversation.

She noted how his eyes roved over her buxom body between bites, resting at the full pout of her lips and the swell of her breasts. If she didn't know him, she might have been flattered. But by the end of dinner, she felt as if she needed to bathe in boiling water to wash away the heat of his gaze.

As soon as the plates were lifted from their settings, she cleared her throat. "If we're finished enjoying ourselves, I'd like to discuss the matter at hand. We have a long journey back tomorrow and it would be best if we could retire early."

She noted the flare of Maksim's nostrils and the tension in his grip as it tightened around his napkin.

"Go on, then."

"As I said, a mermaid was murdered on our shores. Not just any mermaid, a princess."

"And what does this have to do with me?"

"We have reason to believe that one or more of your people are responsible."

His chair grated against stone as he leaned forward, resting his elbows on the obsidian table. "Is that so? And why have you drawn that conclusion?"

"The poison that was used to incapacitate her was created from a plant that resides in your lands. What was the name again, Tolero?"

"The Paratriculus plant, your majesty."

"Ah yes." She pinned Maksim with a sharp brow.

He huffed. "That's all? A plant that anyone could have taken during a visit to Mesantia?" He turned to Tolero, a mocking smile on his face. "Surely you tried to reason with her that this isn't enough to make an accusation?"

Tolero shifted his gaze to her. Heeding their earlier conversation, he remained silent.

"Please direct your questions to me. I'm the one who has final say in this decision. Following our investigation, my council and I concluded that there was sufficient evidence and reasonable motive to bring this to your attention. The manner in which she was murdered was quite brutal, and it's no secret that your people have a strong disdain for the mermaids." She too was now leaning forward on her elbows, matching his posture.

"Many people on this continent have a strong disdain for mermaids. Their siren ancestors have a bloody history with our own." He waved his hand, dismissing the tangent as if it were a throwaway comment.

Celestia's eyes were drawn to Leani who tensed at the cavalier way he spoke of the horrors that had plagued their lands for decades.

He continued, ignoring the offense he caused. "*If* it was one of my people, what would you have me do?" The nonchalance in his voice set her on edge.

"As their ruler, I would expect you to hold them accountable for their crime. They should be made an example of so it doesn't happen again."

"How would you expect me to find this alleged criminal?"

"I thought I was the inexperienced one. You'll, of course, need to launch an investigation, which shouldn't be too difficult seeing as your guards monitor everyone who comes in and out of these gates."

"It doesn't seem worthwhile to put my people through all this trouble for the life of one mermaid. Fortify the gates of your kingdom and guard your beach, and it shouldn't be a problem."

Celestia stood, noisily forcing her chair back a few inches. Tolero and Leani rose in tandem, watching the guards around them as they stepped forward in unison. Her skin took on a bioluminescent glow and her eyes blurred as the magic within her sprang to life, activated by her sudden distress.

"It's your responsibility to be a leader to your people. I suggest you do so. Trust me, I've already fortified my border and security. But I won't back down until you do your part."

Maksim watched her carefully, their eyes locking. His gaze roved over her, taking in the evidence of her power.

"I have a proposition for you." He moved his chair back with the unnatural silence of a predator and began prowling toward her around the long table. "Marry me. Unite our kingdoms. And we can take care of the problem easily. It will likely even resolve itself."

The next time she blinked, he'd appeared in front of her in a swell of mist that resembled thick, mountain fog. She recoiled from him, reaching for her trident that rested against her chair. She forgot he could do that. It wasn't particularly intimidating or powerful magic—he could only use it within his own lands, being that the original source of the Mesantians' power had abandoned them long ago—but the echo of that magic still residing in these mountains was disconcerting.

As he moved even closer, she could see her bioluminescence reflecting off his face as her power surged within her, pushing the glow to the surface of her skin. As she strangled her trident in her grip, trying to keep it at bay, she noticed the tip burning with power as it searched for an outlet. Allowing him to see that she had such little control over her magic would only put her in a more vulnerable position.

"You think that I'd consider marrying you?" Her already large eyes widened in shock. "It's out of the question."

"It would be a smart political move." She hadn't noticed that Tolero had come to her side, but it took everything in her not to snap at him for inserting himself in their conversation.

"You should listen to your advisor. He has many years of experience managing inter-kingdom politics. This could solve problems for both of us."

"And how is that?"

"My people would be your people, making them less inclined to turn against one another. You would also have authority over them, which would help you establish the boundaries you seek. As for my problems, my citizens are running out of resources. The land here is suffering from an increasingly serious drought and recent fires have burned up the greenery and chased off the animals. Having access to the sea would be a great asset and alleviate a lot of their burden—and likely the resentment—that they currently feel."

"The sea's resources belong to the merpeople. You know that was part of the vow I took when I was crowned. I will not be my forefathers and take what doesn't belong to me."

"Are you not the queen of the coastal lands and sea?"

"I am," she said through gritted teeth, "and, as queen, I've decreed that the ocean and all of its resources be returned to them irrevocably. It's always belonged to them, they deserve to thrive and feed their own."

"You have much to learn if you think that's how you rule a kingdom."

"I don't care whether you approve of how I oversee my realm, as we'll never rule together. My answer is no, and I still insist you hold your people accountable, or I'll be forced to take action."

"Is that a threat?" His chest was mere inches from her own as he towered over her.

"It is." She matched his stare, this time allowing the power to swim in her eyes, the prism of cool greens and purples churning with the ebb and flow of her anger.

He searched her gaze, unfamiliar with this side of her. "If you won't marry me and you move to threaten my people, then you leave me with no choice." He gave a flick of his wrist. "Guards, bring her in."

Moments later the doors to the dining hall groaned open, revealing two guards dragging along a woman fighting against them. The first thing Celestia noticed was the lavender hue of her flowing locks and the shimmer of her skin. She wasn't merely a woman; she was a mermaid.

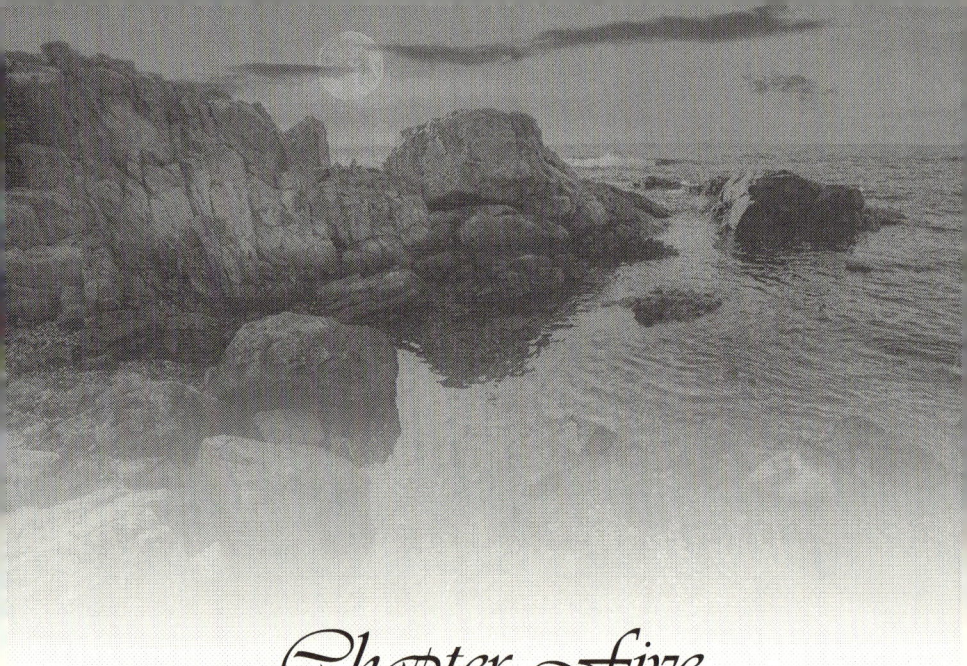

Chapter Five

This all but proved that one of his people killed Estrellia and that he knew about it. Apparently, he had hoped she would drop her pursuit of justice, but when his dismissal wasn't enough to deter her, he played his hand. She had interrupted a much bigger scheme than she'd originally expected.

He only smiled, watching the realization dawn on her—both that he had bigger forces at play than she understood and that he had all the leverage he needed right now.

She had been played the fool.

Celestia had to fight every muscle in her body to keep herself from rushing toward the mermaid being restrained in front of her. But she knew she had to act strategically. Maksim was watching her carefully, daring her to react with violence so he could exact his own.

Celestia looked at Maksim in horror. "You kidnapped a mermaid from my shores?" A murderous impulse ran through her as she fought to contain her anger.

"Did I, personally? No, I did not. But as you see, I have her now, and I will use her to my advantage. If you hadn't been so quick to reject my proposal, perhaps I could have returned her to the sea without anyone knowing, but here we are."

Her breath ceased as her gaze roved over the mermaid whose narrow eyes churned with the same surreal colors that currently swam in Celestia's own. Her lips were a dusty pink, small, but plumply shaped with a deep Cupid's bow. Her eyes dragged over her petite figure, halting abruptly at the legs that followed her slightly rounded hips. There should have been a tail.

She was seething now. "What have you done to her? Why does she have legs?" Her fingers gripped tighter around her trident until her knuckles ached with tension.

A menacing smile crept over his features; the outside finally matched the vileness she knew resided within. "I took her tail away." His eyebrow arched. He was enjoying the leverage that he knew he held.

Celestia fought for control of her rapidly increasing heartbeat. She had come here to seek justice for one fallen mermaid, only to find another being held against her will. She assumed the cuffs were enchanted to quell her magic, otherwise they wouldn't have been able to overpower her.

"Release her. Now." Her voice was deep and steady, her anger radiating within the walls of the dining room.

"No." He clasped his hands in front of his body nonchalantly. "That is, unless you accept my proposal."

"A proposal? Are you out of your mind? You'll be tried for the crimes you committed. You won't be marrying anyone."

"If you so much as attempt any such thing, I will ensure others face the same fate." He only shrugged. "Again, I urge you accept my proposal, Celestia, or things are going to become much more dire in your realm. And as for this one, she won't live to see another day."

Her eyes flicked to the mermaid's. She looked resigned to her capture. Celestia could only assume that she had heard from a young age that humans couldn't be trusted.

"I'd like to call my council. Will you grant me that courtesy?" She gave him a pointed look.

He only nodded, turning on his heel to leave the room. His guards followed close behind, tugging the mermaid rougher than necessary.

Celestia watched every step they took in silence until the heavy door closed with a resounding echo. Finally, she reluctantly turned to face Tolero and Leani.

"Do I have any other options? He can't force me to marry him and allow his transgressions to go unpunished, can he?"

Tolero let out a long sigh. "It would seem so. We're at quite the disadvantage. Unless..." His gaze drifted to Leani momentarily before returning to Celestia's. "Unless you're willing to leave her behind."

Celestia's jaw clenched. The mere suggestion sent a roll of rage through her entire being.

"That's not an option." Her eyes glowed violently as she set them upon him. "As my lead advisor, I would've expected you to understand that only legitimate options are welcome. We don't have time to waste.

There's a woman's life at stake along with our realm's stability."

Tolero rolled his shoulders. "It *is* a legitimate option, you're just too emotional to consider it."

The silence that cut through the room was deafening, not a single breath was released after the words left his lips.

"Tolero, I'm growing weary of your snide remarks and unhelpful opinions. Do not tempt me further to remove you from my council." The edge in her voice was a threat she had long wanted to make.

Tolero's behavior had her on edge lately, and she suspected that she might not be able to trust him to serve her loyally for a while. But now, he remained silent. A wise choice.

"Your majesty, perhaps we could accept his deal." Leani held up a hand when Celestia opened her mouth to protest. "Not in good faith, but as a ruse to free the mermaid and allow us to return to the safety of our kingdom. There, we can formulate a plan that will absolve the promise you make here tonight and ensure he pays for his crimes. He has far too much leverage right now for us to leave here without provoking far worse unless we agree to his terms."

Celestia weighed the potential fallout from such a scheme. It could mean war. But hadn't they, more or less, threatened it either way? She couldn't see any other option to protect everyone in her party, the mermaid included.

The mere thought of being tied—even temporarily—to Maksim turned her stomach. But wasn't this what queens did? Made sacrifices that protected their people? It was the only answer she needed, the clarity of it ringing true.

"We'll do it. I'll begrudgingly accept his proposal… for now." She aimed a sharp look at Tolero, lest he get any ideas. "Once we're back in Cessadia, we'll strategize and find a way out of this engagement."

She breathed deeply, centering herself for the performance she was about to give. "Tolero, let them know we're ready to discuss arrangements."

The party of four followed Tolero back in. Celestia's gaze never left the mermaid as she stumbled to keep up on her foreign limbs.

"So, you've decided to see reason after all. I knew you would." He smiled at Tolero, sharing comradery with whom he expected was the voice of reason.

"Yes, for the good of my people, I'll concede to your request." She didn't need to feign the disgust that fueled her sneer.

He moved closer, placing a palm on her cheek. "Finally, you're thinking like a ruler." His eyes were alight with the power he believed he held over her.

"Release her; she'll stay in my quarters. We'll be leaving in the morning." She stepped back out of his grasp. "We can finalize the details at a later date, I'm not in the mood."

He closed the distance between them abruptly, his hand gripping her chin, the pressure just shy of leaving a bruise. "Don't think you can evade me. You and your kingdom will be mine."

Leani stepped forward, the metallic ringing of her blade cutting through the tension. "Remove your hand at once or lose it." The sword hovered precariously at his wrist.

Maksim's grip loosened, his fingers peeling away. Leani's curved blade followed him as he opened the distance between them once more.

"I'll be seeing you soon." He turned to his guards. "Unchain her." And then he was heading out of the dining hall, temporarily appeased by their agreement.

The woman fell forward when her chains were released, the guards no longer anchoring her upright. Leani was quick enough to catch her before she hit the ground.

She eyed them warily but didn't speak, her petite body rigid in her grasp. Celestia went to help Leani, but when she touched the mermaid, a painful shock ran through her hand. The mermaid jerked away, nearly losing her footing.

Leani looked between them as they stared at one another, none of them understanding what happened. She simply shook her head then looped her arm around the mermaid's waist once more. "I have her, let's just get to our rooms before any more trouble befalls us."

They walked in silence through the dark halls.

Leani bid them goodnight, and then it was just the two of them standing in awkward silence. Celestia swallowed hard under the severe gaze of the mermaid who watched her suspiciously. She knew her aunt's hatred of humans was widespread amongst the merpeople, but she did expect her to have softened toward her somewhat. She supposed it would take time.

"Would you like some fresh clothes? A bath, perhaps?" She offered. Her voice shook with nerves that were not very queenlike. It wasn't just that she'd never been this close to a mermaid, but she was the most beautiful woman she'd ever seen.

The mermaid's eyes darted around the room before answering. "Yes, please." She cleared her throat. Her voice was weak, likely from dehydration. Or perhaps she wasn't used to speaking, merpeople communicated mostly through telepathy, after all.

Celestia rushed to the bedside table where a pitcher of water waited, pouring her a full glass. She held out her hand tentatively. The mermaid grasped the glass, fingers grazing Celestia's. The spark that ignited at the touch caused them both to jump, their eyes raising to one another's in shock.

Celestia swallowed hard. "Why does that keep happening?"

The mermaid shook her head, eyes narrowed—she seemed just as surprised as Celestia was. They stared at one another a moment longer before Celestia went to run the bath, her thoughts racing. When the tub was full, she handed her a towel and clean nightgown. She was slightly embarrassed that all she had to offer was a mere slip of silk, but it would have to do.

"I'll be in the bedroom if you need anything."

The mermaid only nodded before walking on wobbly legs to the bathroom.

When the door shut with a soft click behind her, Celestia threw herself on the bed. The weight of all that had happened in the last few hours melded her into the mattress.

She didn't even hear the door open, or the mermaid get into the bed that could have fit at least four people.

She finally woke hours later and changed her clothes, crawling beneath the covers just in time to fall into a fitful sleep for another few hours. While she wasn't proud of it, she found herself consumed by vivid dreams of the mermaid lying just a few feet away.

Chapter Six

The next time Celestia stirred, the sunrise was shining too brightly through the large windows. She squeezed her eyes shut against the swirls of tangerine, gold, and indigo. She had the urge to fight against the start of a new day, to give into the temptation to return to her dreams, but when she heard Leani's voice, she knew it was no use. Queens didn't get to hide from their responsibilities beneath the covers. As she rallied her energy, she comforted herself with the reminder that the way back was significantly faster since it was downhill.

When she finally threw back the sheets, Celestia was surprised to see the other two women were already dressed.

"Good morning." She sat up, stretching her arms high.

"Good morning. We should get going as soon as possible, preferably before Maksim changes his mind. Aura and I will be out in the stables readying the horses. Meet us there."

Celestia nodded, taking a moment to appreciate the new knowledge of the mermaid's name. "I'll be just a few minutes. I want to get out of here just as badly as you do."

In the shower a few minutes later, she was tempted to stand under the streams of running water for hours. Reluctantly, she turned the water off, letting the cool mountain air that pricked at her skin urge her into motion. She pulled on a pair of black breeches, followed by the metallic mesh undershirt she wore for protection, and a loose-fitting white blouse that would allow her skin to breathe once they descended and traveled back through the heat-stricken lands between here and Cessadia.

After braiding her hair, she gathered her belongings and hastily made her way through the cavernous halls of the palace. Unfortunately, she wasn't fast enough.

In a shroud of mist, Maksim appeared at the entrance, slowly peeling an apple with a small knife. The act made chills run down her spine.

"Were you going to leave without saying goodbye, my lovely betrothed?" The smirk that appeared on his face made her question whether he'd overhead them last night, but she wrote it off as being paranoid.

"I wouldn't dream of it." Her tone was casual, but every muscle in her body was on edge.

He took a bite of the apple, the sound jarring. "I hope you can move past all this 'seeking justice' nonsense."

"It seems I have no choice." Her voice was clipped.

"I'm glad you're thinking clearly, because no matter how much you fortify your borders and guard your shores, if you betray me, the mermaids will pay."

She began her journey to the front gates once again but spun on her heel as a thought occurred to her.

She stepped closer to Maksim, wanting to read his face. "How did you know I would come here, that she would be the key to forcing my hand?"

"That was simply a fortunate intervention of fate. Truly, I hadn't expected you to barge into my realm making demands. I thought it would be the other way around. But now I see you've grown quite bold in our time apart. That's something we'll have to work on if you're to be my wife."

She forced herself to hold her tongue and gave a slight bow of her head, allowing her a moment to swallow her disgust.

"Until next time."

Celestia had thought she made it out unscathed, but then his hand caught her chin just as she passed him, forcing her to meet his gaze. They stared at one another for a moment before he pulled her closer and planted a firm kiss on her lips, scraping the lower half of her pout with his teeth as they separated.

The faint taste of copper filled her mouth as a small cut opened. Every fiber of her being demanded that she rip the dagger from the center of her trident and bury it into his heart, but she knew that wasn't the way to make peace between their kingdoms. Instead, she tried to suppress the revulsion that was growing within her as she wordlessly departed.

Despite all her willpower, tears welled in her eyes as she wiped the tiny dot of blood from her lips. She hated letting him think he had any power over her, but she kept reminding herself it was for the good of the kingdom.

"What happened?" Leani's perceptiveness was part of what made her such a reliable head of her guard—and a loyal friend—but it also meant nothing got past her.

"Nothing. Let's leave. Now." She shrugged her shoulder away as Leani went to pull her closer for inspection. She avoided eye contact with her as she swung herself up onto her horse. She didn't want to see the hurt in her eyes.

Leani cleared her throat. "Aura can't ride on her own, so she'll need to ride with you."

Celestia's gut tightened at the thought of having the mermaid nestled against her for the entire journey home, that mysterious energy endlessly pulsing between them. She fought the heat that crept up the back of her neck and across her cheeks. Distracted by the sudden onslaught of nervous thoughts, she simply nodded and scooted back on her saddle.

Leani hoisted Aura onto the horse. Celestia cautiously reached out her hand to help haul her up, silently praying she didn't receive another harsh shock. This time it seemed they'd both braced for it; the throb of energy they exchanged was powerful but not painful.

As Aura shifted around in the saddle, Celestia tried to ignore the warmth of her soft body pressing into her, lighting up every nerve ending at once. It took all her willpower to resist the urge to lean forward when she smelled like home; crisp, salty air drifted off her wavy lavender locks. She knew then that this was going to be a long ride.

Celestia scooted just slightly, putting space between her chest and Aura's back. Aura turned her head, looking shyly over her shoulder at her, an unspoken question in her eyes. Something about the vulnerability and fear in the mermaid's gaze tugged at her heart strings, urging her to do everything she could to make her more comfortable, even if she was on edge herself.

"I know it feels frightening being up here—even more so for you—but if you hold the pommel here," she took her hand, setting it on the nob at the front of the saddle, "it will help keep you steady."

A concentrated, sharp heat blossomed in her palm as she removed her hand. Aura's eyes widened before she gave her a small smile over her shoulder. The mermaid eagerly gripped onto the pommel with both hands until her knuckles whitened.

Celestia suppressed a laugh and resumed her original spot so that she was providing additional support to keep Aura steady.

They had to wait several more minutes for Tolero to saunter out, chewing the final bites of his breakfast that he'd decided they had time for.

Celestia resisted the urge to roll her eyes.

"How nice of you to join us. I hope you're well fed for our ride." She didn't wait for him to mount before she had her horse trotting off back toward home.

She held the reigns as loosely as possible, trying to avoid physical contact with Aura—a task that seemed impossible as her hands jostled against her thighs every few seconds thanks to the rough terrain. She was so consumed by the overwhelming feeling of all the points their bodies touched that she didn't hear Leani speaking to her at first.

"Celestia?" Leani drew up beside her, tapping her leg to get her attention. "Did you hear me?"

"No, I'm sorry."

Her brow furrowed as she studied her, but she didn't inquire further into her well-being. "I said I don't understand how they could have gotten past the gates, let alone back out with an entire mermaid in tow. A Cessadian must have helped them."

Tolero guffawed. "Or perhaps your guards simply aren't doing their job."

"I will be speaking with them, and if there is a traitor, they will be dealt with. But I trust my guards, I don't think I will find any betrayal on their part."

Celestia nodded, she was confident Leani would uncover the truth. There were other matters to discuss. "I think we need to call a meeting with Meridia first, to see about restoring Aura's tail."

Aura turned to her abruptly, nearly falling from the saddle, but Celestia's arm shot around her, clenching against her waist.

Aura's eyes were wide with fear. "I don't think she'll be able to fix this."

Celestia shared a look with Leani, wondering what Aura could mean, but Tolero interrupted.

"You'll address her as 'Your Majesty' when you speak to the queen." He leveled a glare at Aura.

"*I* will dictate what she calls me." She leaned closer to Aura, whispering in her ear. "You can call me Celestia."

They resumed their journey in tense silence for several minutes before Celestia's curiosity got the better of her irritation.

"What do you mean, Meridia can't fix this?"

"I overheard Maksim talking—bragging really—while he had me held captive. He used magic that your forefathers forbid human access to decades ago. The only place to find what you need is in the book he has—the only known human record of mermaid magic." Aura's sing-song voice wavered. "My fate is in his hands." A single tear dove down her cheek, her iridescent skin making it sparkle. It was beautiful, but it also threatened to break Celestia's heart. She seemed so resigned to her loss.

"We'll figure it out. I promise." She gripped her hand reassuringly. Tolero snorted.

"You doubt your queen's word?" Celestia threw her voice to reach Tolero who rode just ahead of her.

"I don't think that even the queen can conjure unknown magic to fix a problem she doesn't fully understand."

Celestia's shoulders tensed. She was nearly at her wit's end with him. "I never said I could, but I can ensure that he is forced to give me what I need to restore her tail."

The next few hours were mostly spent in silence, the breeze picking up and whipping debris and sand around them, effectively drowning out their voices anytime they did try to start conversation.

Since they were on a decline, and the temperatures were much cooler heading back, they were able to make better time. When they finally saw the shell-encrusted gates, Celestia nearly fell from her horse in relief as the tension of the last few days flooded from her body. The sound of the crashing waves and the sight of the palace glimmering with the evening lights beckoned to her, urging her forward with the last of her remaining energy.

Chapter Seven

As soon as they'd arrived at the castle, Celestia got Aura settled in the suite next door and immediately went to sleep. She'd been far too exhausted to care about how dirty she was from being exposed to the elements. But she took her time in the bath the next morning. Fortunately, she had another hour until she needed to make her way to the throne room to meet with her council.

She allowed herself to indulge in the little amount of power she did have control of, forcing a few small droplets of bath water to shape-shift and rise in the air. As a child, it had been a way to entertain herself. Now it was a way to evaluate her abilities—however minimal they were. She suspected that was because she lived on land, and, based on what she knew, mermaid magic primarily relied on water—at least for larger feats. Yes, she had greater strength and the bioluminescence of her aquatic relatives, but with limited access to the enchanted waters—it wasn't as if she could carry it around with her on land—her powers were quite limited.

When her fingers and toes began to prune, she knew it was time to quit playing and get ready.

As she was tying off the final laces of her dress, a knock announced a visitor.

"Come in."

Her heart leaped out of her chest when Aura peeked through, taking tentative steps into the room. Her eyes darted around in awe, taking in the various chandeliers and golden embellishments that adorned her high ceilings. Celestia had spent years getting the room just right. It was lavish, but it was where she took her solace from the demands of her life. Her favorite part was the open balcony that allowed the ocean breeze and the crash of waves to float in at all hours of the day.

"Did you sleep well?"

Aura nodded as she twisted her fingers nervously through her lilac hair that hung loosely around her shoulders and down her waist. Her eyes now roamed over Celestia. As the mermaid's gaze lingered, she resisted the urge to fidget under her silent appraisal.

She was wearing one of her favorite dresses. The sheer aqua fabric ran snugly down the generous curves of her body, slightly flaring out toward the bottom. Gold chains adorned her neck, crossing her chest and looping around her shoulders, creating a decorative harness.

She wasn't sure if she imagined it, but Aura's cheeks seemed to redden briefly.

Celestia turned, fighting her nerves as she picked up her crown from its cushion and placed it atop her thick, tousled waves, where it sat comfortably. Despite the ornate shells and gems, the golden metal wire that made up the underlying structure took the brunt of the weight.

Aura bowed her head slightly. "Your Majesty."

Celestia couldn't help the way her heart and stomach fluttered in unison at the admiration in her tone.

"Call me Celestia, please. Especially in private." She reached out, tilting Aura's chin up and raising her back to full height. The slight touch sent that current through her but instead of making her want to recoil, it drew her closer.

Before she knew what she was doing, her fingers moved of their own volition, gently tucking a pastel strand behind Aura's ear.

She could hear the mermaid swallow thickly.

"Celestia, I wanted to thank you for rescuing me. I didn't expect to make it out of there whole or free, and then you came."

"You don't owe me any thanks, I only did what was right. They shouldn't have been able to capture you at all. That was my failing."

The mermaid closed the distance between them, looking up at her through thick lashes. Her gaze searched Celestia's intently, as if she were looking for an anchor to tether her trust.

Celestia dared not move an inch, hoping she could convey everything she wanted to say in her gaze. She couldn't explain it, but since the first time she set eyes on the mermaid, all she wanted was to be close to her. She yearned to touch her, to hear the sound of her voice, to take comfort in another of her kind.

The longer they stood there, the more it felt like there was some magnetic force pushing and pulling between them. And then Aura blinked.

She noticed the swirling colors in the mermaid's eyes slowing and it made sense. Aura had been using her siren song on her, but she wasn't sure why. Her brow furrowed with concern.

As if reading her mind, the words poured out of the mermaid. "I'm sorry, I shouldn't have. Sometimes it just starts to happen before I know what's going on. I promise I wasn't trying anything, Your Majesty." Again, her head bowed.

She nodded, but even when Aura had stopped, there was still something between them—another force at work that'd been there since the day the met. Something much more subtle and enduring. Celestia felt uneasy, but she also believed that Aura didn't have bad intentions. There was still so much she had to learn about mermaids, which was a failing on her part as queen, but it had always been so painful to uncover their wondrous ways when she was kept out of it. Always so "other," despite the few gifts bestowed on her at birth.

"Celestia" she corrected her. "It's okay, I know you didn't mean any harm." She rubbed her hand over the colorful scales on her arm nervously. "Can I ask you something?"

Aura met her gaze, eyes churning with curiosity. "Of course."

"What was that? I mean, why does it happen?" She found herself winding a green strand around her finger.

She noted how Aura's cheeks flushed pink before she spoke.

"It's a survival instinct passed on from our siren ancestors. It's an alluring magic that takes over when we have the urge to… possess something, or someone. It's meant to help draw humans to us."

She shifted nervously on her feet and avoided eye contact, as if she would rather be doing anything other than having this conversation.

Celestia stepped forward, closing the distance between them, and dared to run her fingers through the mermaid's silken hair, gently palming the back of her neck, the heat of magic throbbing just there. "Aura, are you trying to lure me in? Because you don't need magic to do that. I feel it too, this inexplicable pull between us. And I don't think it has anything to do with the siren song."

As she drew even closer, her eyes set on the mermaid's plump lips, she heard the knob of her bedroom door turn.

"Your Majesty, you're late. I just wanted to make sure everything was okay." Tolero's shifty eyes flicked between Celestia and Aura, a knowing sneer played upon his lips. "We should go."

Celestia gathered her composure, pulling her shoulders back and steeling her face.

"Let's go then."

She wouldn't give Tolero the satisfaction of appearing guilty, her engagement to Maksim wasn't real, so what she was doing wasn't wrong. Even though she repeated the sentiment to herself several times, she still worried about how he would use the information to his advantage.

Celestia followed closely on his heels but chanced a small wave to Aura when she broke away from their group to return to her suite.

As they entered the throne room, Celestia cast away the events of the morning and the fluttering of her stomach.

With every step up to the throne, her focus sharpened. They had a marriage to avoid, a crime to get justice for, and an angry merqueen waiting for them. There was no time for distractions if she wanted them all to come out of the other side of this with peace intact.

She closed her eyes, counted to three, and, when she opened them again, she was ready to do her duty.

The energy was tense amongst the council as they gathered that morning, and it only escalated as the minutes ticked by. After an hour of deliberation, they were no closer to a safe way out of her engagement with Maksim, or a way to hold him accountable for his crimes against the merpeople. He was in for a real surprise if he thought she was just going to let him get away with his atrocities, even if they didn't have a solution just yet.

Everyone was too focused on handling the immediate issue that was looming just off the shore—Meridia.

Her aunt was known for her wrath and fierce hatred for humans. When she found out that there was further harm done to the merpeople and that they'd failed to make any progress, she would let it all out on Celestia and, worse, possibly send a raging storm onto their shores.

She knew she shouldn't be afraid of her, but the truth of it was that there was no way around it. Meridia was a powerful mermaid with magic that instilled fear in all those who had heard of her.

While she was fairly confident that she wouldn't drown them in a fifty-foot wave since they did bring Aura back, she knew that Meridia would let her know what a failure she was. That she was useless in protecting her people. And the severity with which she would deliver that fact would leave Celestia reeling as much as any physical wound.

But there was no avoiding it. She allowed herself a moment to breathe in the salty air before she descended the castle steps with her council in tow. Each step that closed the distance between her and the sea ratcheted up her anxiety.

She had asked Aura to stay behind for now, under the guise that she was recovering. But the fact of the matter was that Celestia knew her aunt would be much harsher if she could physically see the harm that had come to one of her own. One of Meridia's only redeeming qualities—if you asked Celestia—was her fierce protectiveness of the merpeople.

When they reached the shoreline there was no one around, but she knew Meridia would be there soon. Mermaid magic allowed them to sense when their kin were near, a silent call that only they could feel.

Within minutes, Meridia emerged on the surface, bobbing in the current as close as she could get without the water being too shallow.

"Celestia."

She tried not to let it bother her that Meridia refused to address her by her royal title. It wouldn't do to walk into this with hostility if there was any hope for them to work together to find a solution for Aura. She simply returned the gesture.

"Meridia. I have news from Mesantia." She watched her estranged aunt's eyes tighten in response. "I have evidence that King Maksim knew about the murder and may have even ordered it himself."

She paused, allowing Meridia to sit with the information before continuing.

"And there's more… he took a mermaid prisoner as well."

Meridia's face contorted with rage, the sea responding with a dangerous current that churned the water feverishly.

"How did his men breach your gates in the first place? You are supposed to protect your people."

"We don't know. We've spoken to all of our guards, none of which have raised our suspicions."

"How reassuring. And let me guess, you were unable to free her?"

"She's at the castle, recovering from her injuries." Celestia let out a long sigh, dread threatening to drown her from within as she worked up the courage to say the words she knew would horrify her. "They used magic on her. They replaced her tail with legs."

Meridia surged forward a few feet, rearing her body up above the water. She knew she couldn't leave the sea, but every muscle in Celestia's body tensed, ready to flee.

"How did you let this happen? You were supposed to keep us safe. That was the agreement." Her fist slammed down into the water creating a violent splash that coated her damp skin in droplets. "Do you have any idea what this means?"

Celestia shook her head, her muscles so taut that it was barely a movement.

"They have access to power that endangers us all. And you've given them the confidence to do so."

"That's not fair. I'm learning as fast as I can. You're the one who refuses to provide council, leaving me here to deal with the mess after my father died."

Her anger was unabated now. She wouldn't let this all rest on her shoulders. She could feel the magic coursing through her, could see the water's edge tugging closer to her in response. Meridia's eyes sharpened at the sight, but no one commented on it. Instead, Celestia did her best to stifle it, even as she began glowing. It wouldn't help anything if Meridia felt threatened. She needed to keep her wits about her.

"We are looking for a solution, and I will find one. I just need time."

Meridia eyed her carefully. "You don't have time, do you? Something else is going on that you haven't told me, something that has you more on edge than usual."

"I can manage. I'll come back when I have an update. In the meantime, I'll be keeping the coast heavily guarded, but can you order the mermaids to stay away from the shore and out of the coves?"

Meridia nodded, her expression stern.

Celestia dared to ask the question hanging tensely between them. "How did you not know one of your own was missing?"

Meridia turned her head, not wanting to admit her oversight. "There are thousands of us living in these waters, I can't possibly keep track of every single one of them." Her brow furrowed. "I should have known though. Our territory has a magical boundary, if anyone tries to leave, my magic would have alerted me. But if they took her at the same time they killed Estrellia, I may have been too distracted by the pain of her death to notice."

"There's no changing what happened, we can only find a solution for what's been done."

Celestia signaled to her council that it was time to go. She hadn't made it more than a few steps before her aunt's voice called over her shoulder.

"Come back tomorrow at noon. I think I have a way to help."

Celestia didn't respond, but she had a sense of deep foreboding about what kind of solution Meridia was offering and what the cost would be.

Chapter Eight

When Celestia returned to her room, she let all the pressure of the last few days evacuate her body through her tears. She was drowning in the stress and guilt of all that had happened. It was her responsibility to protect these people, and she kept failing them.

She ripped the crown from her head and tossed it across the bed in disgust. Right now, she didn't feel worthy of wearing it. Its weight was a reminder of her ineptitude.

When she finally reigned in her sobs, she readied herself for dinner. Luckily, Allora had heard her and brought by some cooled cucumbers for her eyes to help bring down the swelling and refresh her before she needed to put on a brave face.

It would just be her, the council, and some favored members of court who were visiting the castle, but she couldn't afford to show any weakness. Any doubt in their minds could easily open Cessadia to threats. While they all presented as confidants and friends, she had learned early on in her queendom that appearances could be deceiving. Everyone had their own interests to protect, and they would do so without hesitation.

While she was dreading a night of politicking, she was also looking forward to seeing Aura.

Tolero had shared the details of her capture and subsequent release, and now everyone was clamoring to meet a mermaid in the flesh.

The thought of putting Aura on display like some kind of oddity made her stomach turn, but Leani assured her that she had spoken with Aura, who had agreed to attend despite the awkward circumstances.

And Celestia was excited to have her there. She craved her attention, her soft smiles, and the way the colors in her eyes brightened with interest when she looked at her. With Aura by her side, her night would be infinitely better.

She felt a pull to the mermaid that she couldn't quite explain, but she knew part of it was that her quiet and calm demeanor was comforting to Celestia, who was always surrounded by domineering people vying for power. Except for Leani of course; Leani was always her rock to lean on. And for that, she was thankful. She wouldn't have made it this far without her.

As if she had been summoned by Celestia's thoughts, Leani appeared at the door. A genuine smile met her in the reflection and some of the tension instantly eased from her shoulders.

"Are you holding up okay?"

Celestia met her gaze in the mirror, shrugging. "I don't have any other choice."

"The weight of royalty has never been good for anyone's peace of mind." Leani stepped inside, revealing a cup of her calming tea, Celestia's favorite.

"Have I ever told you I love you?" She smiled as the mint and herbs danced across her tongue.

Finishing off the delicious dregs of the tea, she breathed in and out several times like Leani had taught her as a child when she needed to calm herself. When she opened her eyes again, she felt more confident that she could handle what this night had in store. With her resolve settling within her, she stood, making the short walk over to the pillar where her evening crown sat.

Having multiple crowns had always seemed pretentious to Celestia, but, now that she was queen, she understood just how important appearances were.

Leani took it from her hands gently—admiring the gleaming opals and pearls that sat amongst beautiful shells and crystals—before carefully setting it atop her head.

"Stunning as always, my queen."

Celestia laughed. "Will you ever stop with that nonsense?"

"No. Especially not in times like these when you need to be reminded just how powerful you are."

Celestia fought the tears that welled in her eyes and pulled Leani into a firm hug that reminded her that she did still have allies in this castle, even if they were few and far between lately.

"Thank you." She squeezed her hand one time before putting on her last pieces of jewelry—a large dangling pair of gold earrings that were encrusted with opals and diamonds and a matching ring.

"Is Aura ready?"

"Yes. I told her to remain in her room until we came for her. I didn't want Tolero or any of those other vultures to get their talons in her."

Celestia nodded seriously, sudden worry for Aura's well-being churning her stomach until it felt more turbulent than the waters that crashed against the rocks outside her window.

Celestia went to knock on Aura's door, but her hand froze mid-air, nerves getting the better of her. Leani gave her a knowing look, her smirk growing wide. It was enough to force her hand to move, rapping against the wood three times.

"Who is it?"

"It's Celestia, you can open up, it's safe."

The door creaked open slowly as Aura revealed a sliver of her face. Her caution was warranted, but it still made Celestia's chest tighten that she still didn't feel safe.

"Are you ready?"

Aura only nodded, anxiety weighing down her features, but she was as beautiful as ever. Her long, lavender hair fell in waves around her waist, her skin glimmered as the moonlight seeped in from the large, open arches, and the brilliant shades of emerald, sapphire, and amethyst danced in her eyes. The blush hue of the gown she had selected complimented her soft demeanor perfectly.

One look at her stole the breath right out of Celestia's chest. She had to remember how to exhale when her gaze locked with Aura's.

If Leani hadn't been there, she didn't even know if she would have made it to dinner, she was content to stand here for eternity looking upon the stunning creature before her.

"Let's go ladies, nothing good comes from allowing bored nobles to gossip for too long."

Celestia rolled her eyes but turned to leave, holding her hand out for Aura to take. Her warm grasp was the only reassurance she needed that she had to go in there with her head held high and take control of the situation.

When they entered the dining hall, she noted that everyone was still standing and mingling, as was custom until the king or queen arrived. At the very least, they respected her enough to honor tradition. However, she didn't miss how all eyes fell on her when she entered hand-in-hand with Aura. The sounds of excited voices immediately fell to a deafening silence.

She could feel Aura pull against her, seeking to free her hand, but Celestia intercepted her, linking their arms. She rested her other hand on the mermaid's, reassuring her that she wasn't letting her out of her sight. Not in this crowd.

She took a seat in her high-backed chair at the end of the table and gestured for Leani to take the seat on her left, while Aura took the one on her right. She wanted to keep them both close. She would need to draw on their comfort and strength.

At least the meal itself was warm and enjoyable, even if the majority of her company wasn't.

She allowed herself the small joy of watching Aura out of the corner of her eye as she reveled in all the new flavors she was experiencing. It was much sweeter than any dessert the chef could have prepared.

And then there was the sparkling wine. Celestia tried not to smirk when she noticed how Aura carefully watched the bubbles that danced in her glass, or how her eyes went wide when they tickled her tongue and throat. However, she couldn't stop her mind from imagining how much sweeter the aged wine would be if she were to taste it from the mermaid's perfectly curved lips.

Everything Aura did held Celestia's attention, and after a while she couldn't help but fantasize what it would be like if she and Aura were here together, as queen and queen. She knew it was absurd to be thinking such a thing when she barely knew her, but the thought took hold in her mind and wouldn't let up, and then her heart joined in too, nearly bursting with desire.

Celestia was broken from her thoughts by the grating sound of Tolero's voice. What she wouldn't give to banish that man to another realm.

She steeled herself from allowing her annoyance to show, pasting on the patient smile she'd trained herself in so well, before turning her full attention to him.

Noting that she hadn't heard him the first time, he repeated himself. "I suppose congratulations are in order."

Celestia's brow creased, unsure of where this was headed.

"Your engagement." A knowing smile dragged his lips up as he studied her before turning his attention to the guests. "You'll all be happy to know that our queen has accepted a proposal of marriage from King Maksim of Mesantia."

The moment the word 'proposal' left his lips everything else faded out. Her ears were ringing, blackness crept into the sides of her vision, and anger was such a violent force within her that she was shaking. Until she felt a warm touch on her arm. Then everything came rushing back into focus.

"Celestia," Aura whispered softly so only she could hear. "Stay here with me. Just smile. It'll be okay." She gave her one more squeeze before returning her hand to her lap, keeping a carefully placed smile on her face the whole time. She learned quickly.

Celestia did her best to calm the thrum of power rolling through her that demanded Tolero's head on the end of her trident.

No one was supposed to know about the engagement. It wasn't even real. How could he have done this to her? Now, when it was inevitably called off, it would cause so many more problems for her. Celestia's fingers twitched with the desire to thrust her trident across the room, directly into his heart.

She curled her hands into fists at the table, before reminding herself that she should be pretending to be excited about the engagement in front of all these important dinner guests.

"Thank you, Tolero, for sharing the exciting news." Her voice was tight, and she had to force her vocal cords to loosen before she kept speaking. "Maksim and I were hoping to announce it at the upcoming ball, but now is as good a time as any, I suppose."

Tolero's eyes glinted with satisfaction. She would admit that he had out maneuvered her in this instance, but she would not be made a fool. And he'd done her a favor. He'd confirmed that he was indeed the threat she thought he was, and she now had the validation she needed to get rid of him. She allowed herself comfort in that fact while she struggled to keep the smile on her face and the sparkle in her eyes as she joined in a toast.

Chapter Nine

$\mathcal{T}$he rest of the evening had passed far too slowly for Celestia's liking. She was drained the next morning, and, as she waited for Tolero to enter the throne room, she found herself flexing her jaw trying to work out the soreness from hours of fake smiling.

While she was irritable, she found some joy in the fact that she was finally going to be rid of Tolero. She even dressed for the occasion in a dramatic, gauzy, black dress that looked like she'd swept in from the underworld. Celestia never wore black, but it seemed fitting.

When he finally graced her with his presence, he quickly became aware that it wasn't an emergency council meeting as she'd claimed. There was no denying that things were looking dire for him when he was surrounded by her guards, and Celestia was shooting daggers at him from where she hovered above on her throne.

She arched a high brow as he stood there, unwilling to begin until he bowed. She would do everything in her power to make him feel as frustrated as she was before dismissing him. It was only fair, after all.

He was stubborn, but she didn't relent with her disdainful gaze until he complied. When he stood again, his eyes were dark pits of hatred.

"Tolero, I've called you here today-"

"Are all the dramatics necessary, Celestia?" He raised his hands, gesturing at the room around them.

"That's *Your Highness* to you, and, yes, it's necessary because I deem it so." She shifted forward so she was leering down at him. "What you did last night was not only reckless, it was in deliberate violation of the orders I gave you. You've put us at unnecessary risk, and, for that, you will be stripped of your title and dismissed from council."

"That's absurd, you can't do this. I've been as much a ruler of this kingdom as you have. We wouldn't be where we are today without me. I refuse."

"We wouldn't be where we are… well, yes, I believe that's correct. We have citizens being murdered, threats coming in from other kingdoms, and what have you done other than try to dismiss and undermine me every step of the way?"

"Your father would be so disappointed in you. You've disgraced your crown and will run this kingdom into the depths before your reign is over." He was so angry that spittle was flying from his twisted lips.

Celestia took a deep, centering breath before she stood and grabbed her trident. Her guards took a synchronized step forward as she descended the steps of the throne. She stopped about a foot away from Tolero. Her trident made a sharp sound as she slammed its base on the ground. She wanted to see his face crumple when he realized he was done for.

"Leave now with some of your dignity intact, or I'll have my guards drag you out. Your choice."

His face was mottled and red as he stared her down, likely trying to think of a threat that would force her hand.

"You'll ruin this kingdom by putting those creatures first. You're putting your people at risk while you lavish your attention on that girl. But don't listen to me, you'll see for yourself the grave price of your mistakes soon enough."

"Out. Now." She was glowing violently with power, casting a blue gleam around the room.

"Guards, see that all of his belongings are removed from the castle immediately and ensure that everyone knows he's not allowed back in."

With that, she left Tolero in the throne room for her guards to contend with.

Celestia unlaced the tight, black dress, struggling with its excessive amount of fabric. When she finally freed herself, standing in the simplicity of her slip was blissful. She breathed a sigh of relief, going over to the breakfast tray of scones and berries that Allora had thoughtfully left for her.

She popped a strawberry in her mouth, gazing out at the waves, which reminded her she needed to meet her aunt soon to learn more about the mysterious solution she was offering.

She sighed deeply before going over to her wardrobe to select something that would better tolerate sea mist and sand. After short deliberation, she selected a flowy, blush garment. Once her hair was loosely braided and her crown was secured in place, she quickly made her way through the pristine halls of the palace.

The walk from her suite to the beach was far too quick for Celestia's liking as dread pooled in her stomach. It felt like she'd had no time at all to mentally prepare herself before the salty breeze was assaulting her senses. Celestia removed her shoes as soon as her toes hit the sand, enjoying how the warmth and softness centered her. For a minute, she simply allowed herself to focus on the peaceful sound of the waves. But then she felt her.

Meridia didn't need to say anything as she rose from the depths, gleaming, silvery-white hair clinging to her shapely figure.

Without any greeting, Meridia charged ahead. "Based on what you've told me, I can only assume that Maksim is working with someone who has intimate knowledge of old magic that your father promised would be safe in his keeping. Apparently, that was a lie, but it doesn't matter anymore. What's done is done." She let out a disappointed sigh. "As much as we have our differences, forcing Maksim to submit is in both of our best interests, and it's necessary to keep the merpeople safe. I was able to create this for you." Something dangled from her grasp.

Celestia tentatively walked into the waves, stopping just inches from Meridia. It was the closest she'd ever been to her. She couldn't help but linger on the familial traits she recognized from pictures of her mother. Those large, moonstone eyes, full lips, voluptuous curves, and the otherworldly beauty. But what was drastically different was their demeanor. Her mother was known for being gentle and kind, despite being forced into a marriage and away from her home. Meridia was hateful and wrathful, her eyes always squinting suspiciously, and her lips twisted in irritation.

"What is it?" She asked skeptically.

"It's an enchanted bracelet. Each bead holds the ability to cast one protection spell using the water inside"

Celestia took it from her aunt's outstretched hand, careful not to touch her too intimately. She held it up for closer inspection; an entire ocean swam inside each bead. She was transfixed by the crystal blue water and lively waves that raged within.

"How does it work?" Her voice was awestruck.

"When you need to use it, remove a single bead by summoning it to you. Clasp the bead in your hand and picture exactly what you want to happen. But, keep in mind, this is mermaid magic, meaning whatever spell you cast must use the force of water."

"And it just comes?"

"Yes. The enchanted water will respond because you have your ancestors' magic within you. You've struggled with your power for this long because you don't have full access to the water, but now you do. You simply need to learn to wield it."

Celestia knew she had magic, she could feel it thrumming within her often, see the pulsing glow of it on her skin, could play with it in small, rare bouts, but she'd never been shown how to truly harness it, so she was forced to keep it at bay. Her father had tried to teach her a few things about how to contain it—likely so she didn't accidentally hurt anyone. Meridia was greedy with what help she would dole out, even if it would help keep her niece and the kingdom safe.

"But how—"

Her aunt's brow slammed down as her head whipped toward the shore, a grimace on her face. Celestia turned to see what had disturbed her so.

It was Aura. Her lips formed a deep pout, and her brow was furrowed in worry.

Celestia rushed toward the shore, forcing her body to fight through the strong waves that seemed to pull her back with more intent than usual.

"What are you doing out here?" Worry ate at her stomach, turning the scones and berries she'd eaten earlier.

"I wanted to talk to you."

Celestia didn't answer. Instead, she turned her attention back to the waves and Meridia. She couldn't miss the sheer disgust that burdened her features. Celestia had been on the receiving end of that look countless times, but she wouldn't allow it to be directed at Aura. She shifted protectively in front of her, shielding her from the brunt of her aunt's disdain.

That only made Meridia angrier.

"Fix this," she hissed as she turned to dive back into the water.

"Wait!" Celestia hated that she needed Meridia's help but she was right, it was in both of their best interests. "How am I supposed to learn how to harness my magic? I'm hardly in control of it."

Meridia didn't even turn around fully, just grunted out over her shoulder, "Ask her." And then she was gone, the tip of her pearlescent, silver tail flipping up water behind her.

Celestia blew out a frustrated breath, turning to Aura. She searched her face for sadness or discomfort, but the mermaid's features were calm and controlled.

Aura lifted a hand to her shoulder, squeezing once. "I'll help you. While I might have limited access to my power on land, I have enough to teach you how to hone it."

Celestia couldn't help the bright smile that spread across her face at the thought of spending more time with her.

She wrapped her arm around Aura's elbow as they turned toward the castle. She found that she now took comfort in the odd sensation that struck every time they touched—even seeking it out—and it seemed Aura did too. It was a reminder that she was here, even if it was temporary.

On their walk back, they decided they should start lessons immediately. They only had a few days, at most, to help Celestia learn to harness and wield her powers.

Chapter Ten

Celestia grunted in irritation. Sweat coated her brow and the back of her neck, so much so that her hair was starting to frizz. She yanked it up in a voluminous ponytail, relieving a smidge of frustration when she pulled it taut.

Aura winced at the hint of aggression but sat patiently as Celestia regained her composure.

She took a deep breath and repeated it two more times for good measure.

"Okay, let's go again."

"We should take a break, you haven't had enough sleep and calling on your magic can take a lot out of you."

"We don't have time for me to be well rested," Celestia said a little too sharply.

They had been at this almost incessantly since they left the beach, but she knew Aura shouldn't be on the receiving end of her frustration.

"I'm sorry. I appreciate your help, I do. I just want to master this so I can protect my people—our people."

Aura rested her delicate hands on her shoulders. "You can, and you will." The determination in her gaze lit a fire within Celestia, she had never seen the mermaid so sure of anything.

"Now, close your eyes and imagine all of the water in the ocean rushing to you. When you call on it, don't be commanding like you're trying to be its master. The ocean is a creature all its own and demands respect. Instead, call to it by opening yourself up, allowing it to find a home in you."

Celestia felt ridiculous, but Aura was the expert. In her mind's eye, she pictured tall waves moving at a fierce speed, coming straight to her without any resistance as she removed another bead. Her eyes shot open as a feeling of fullness swam through her. Her palms and the space between her eyes were tingling as if the power now rested there. When she looked down, she was glowing more brightly than ever before, and her entire body was trembling with newfound strength. She looked up to see a restless body of water swirling around them, just as she'd willed.

Aura's lips were parted but she didn't speak. Instead, she rushed to the dresser and grabbed the small, handheld mirror that rested there, shoving it in front of Celestia. Her mouth hung open at her reflection. Her eyes were churning moonstone, her skin was glowing a fierce, bioluminescent blue, and the center of her forehead was illuminated with the power pulsing steadily there. Every ounce of power she'd seen within herself before paled to this; it was as if she was lit from within. She fought the urge to flinch away from the force growing inside of her.

Aura held her steady, her arms wrapped around her shoulders and her chin nestled in the crook of Celestia's neck. "Embrace it. There's nothing to fear. This is the truest form of who you are. You've never looked more beautiful, Celestia."

At those words, power danced across her skin, bursting from her.

Aura moved in front of her, grasping one hand and then the other, raising their palms together. There was a current raging between them. It pulsated as Aura gently stroked down the center of her palms, sending a strong vibration throughout Celestia's body. It was as if their powers were mingling together. Was this the phantom spark she'd been feeling all along, their powers communicating?

A mesmeric force washed over her, clouding her mind of anything but Aura—of embracing her, of the feel of her lips against her own, of tasting her. The allure drew Celestia forward inch by inch like an invisible tether. They shared one hesitant breath before their lips clashed together, and all she saw was an explosion of stars.

She found herself urging Aura back into the chair, one hand planted firmly on the oversized armrest to hold her steady, the other wrapping around her waist to meld their bodies together.

Aura's hands cradled her face, her touch featherlight as always, but there was no missing the passion of her lips and tongue caressing Celestia's own.

She could feel their hearts beating excitedly in tandem as they allowed themselves to act on the desire that had been growing between them.

When Aura broke away, resting her forehead against Celestia's, she could feel the current recede beneath her skin. As it did, her mind began to clear, and she couldn't help but read Aura's expression as regret.

"Was that the siren song?" Celestia backed away, giving her some distance.

Aura shook her head and when she lifted her eyes, there were tears threatening to break free.

"No. That was… us."

"Then why do you look like you regret it?"

"I don't."

Celestia didn't want to push her, but she also needed to know she wasn't the only one feeling this connection. She tucked a strand of Aura's lavender hair behind her ear. "Be honest with me, please. Do you want this?" She closed her eyes, casting a wish into the universe for whoever was listening.

"Yes." It was barely audible, but the quiet confirmation breathed new life into every inch of Celestia's body and soul.

She leaned forward, determined to feel the soft caress of her lips again, but Aura turned away.

"Our magic is telling us this is meant to be but, in reality, we could never be anything. I don't understand." Her voice was tight with unshed tears.

"What do you mean?" Celestia tried to keep the eagerness out of her voice. She knew this was all happening too fast, but she couldn't deny how right it felt.

"As mermaids, our magic alerts us when we've found our soulmate. It's old magic that helped us survive centuries of existing, spread out across open seas." She released a deep sigh. "You know that spark you feel between us when we touch…"

Celestia only nodded. Hopefulness and doubt were battling inside her as Aura explained power she didn't understand but desperately wanted to believe in.

"That's the sign. That's our bond, pulling us toward one another. With each touch, our powers bind us more closely. Every time we indulge it, our souls weave tighter together." The expression on her face was pained. "And now, when we inevitably part, it'll be like our souls are ripped in two, because this…" she gestured between them, "cannot be, and the fates are very cruel."

"If ancient magic says so, then there must be a way." Being a dreamer had left Celestia disappointed over and over again, but she believed in Aura. She believed in them, together.

"How?" Aura leaned back, her head braced against the wall, defeat in her eyes. "You're human, I'm a mermaid who lives in the sea… at least I hope I will again soon. Not to mention, you're a queen and I'm not of noble blood. And that's not even considering that you're currently betrothed."

Aura began to flit about the room on anxious feet. In her short time on legs, she'd picked up the habit of pacing.

Celestia used her magic to send the swirling water away, forcing it over the balcony and out into the ocean. She was exhausted now, and it was too loud.

"You'll get your tail back. I promise." Celestia stopped her mid-step, putting her hands on her shoulders. "The rest of it doesn't matter. I'm the queen, I make the rules. And Maksim? He'll never be my husband."

Celestia walked over to the bed and lay back, rolling on her side. A tug of Aura's hand had her crawling up beside her. Her proximity and calming demeanor were what she needed most right now.

Celestia closed her eyes and inhaled deeply, the saltwater scent chasing worries of Maksim from her mind for the moment.

She forced herself to focus only on Aura's closeness, her silence more comforting than the cheers and praise of a hundred subjects.

"Do you really believe there's no way to make this work?"

"I don't see how it can. But, truthfully, I'm not so sure of anything anymore." The wistfulness in her tone forced Celestia's eyes open.

As the first hopeless tear fell, Celestia's lips caught it against her cheek. She followed them lower, placing a soft kiss on her lush lips. When Aura's breathing evened once again, she leaned her forehead against hers and reveled in the steadiness of her heartbeat, the warmth of her breath, and the safety of her embrace.

If they couldn't have forever, then she would at least make the most of the time they had now. Before she drifted off to sleep, she told herself that she would spend every free moment she had showing Aura all that they could have if she were just brave enough to dream with her.

Chapter Eleven

Hours had passed when Celestia woke from her unexpected nap, the sun now setting. She jumped up, hurrying to get ready for the emergency council meeting she had called.

She slipped on a simple, pale-green gown and a lightweight, silver-threaded cape, finishing the ensemble with her evening crown. As she swiped some color on her lips, Aura began to rouse.

Before she woke too fully, Celestia rushed over to her, holding her hand gently.

"You can stay. I have a council meeting, but it shouldn't take more than an hour or two. Make sure you're rested. When I get back, I have somewhere I want to take you."

She placed a kiss on her forehead, grabbed her trident out of its stand, and strode down the long halls toward the throne room.

The council was already waiting for her when she arrived. As soon as she planted herself on the throne, the questions came flying.

"How could you dismiss Tolero? He's served this kingdom longer than any of us!" Borris, another long-time council member from her father's reign, was on his feet.

"I understand that it may seem jarring. However, Tolero has shown that his loyalty wavers on several occasions. He couldn't be trusted to do what's right for this kingdom." She instilled firmness in her tone, hoping for swift acceptance.

"In your opinion," he spat back.

"Yes, in my opinion, which is based on years of evidence. Decision after decision, Tolero has undermined me, and his decision to reveal the engagement to Maksim—against my instruction and our mutual agreement, might I add—put all of us at risk. He's been playing a dangerous game and I won't allow his reckless behavior and prejudices to compromise my people's safety any longer."

Borris only scoffed.

Before his thighs hit the seat, she unsettled him with a warning. "Borris, you would do well to remember that I demand respect inside and outside of my throne room. If you no longer wish to serve on my council, you need only resign." She leveled an unflinching gaze at him before addressing the group.

"Tolero's dismissal may cause some concern amongst our citizens. If they approach you, you're to reassure them that his leaving was a security measure and that we have everything under control." She smoothed the silk of her dress. "And if anyone questions you about Maksim, confirm the engagement but don't give them any details."

She looked to Leani, who would deliver the next bit of news.

"We need to present a united front for now. Maksim will be expecting Celestia to make a formal commitment to their engagement soon, so we'll be holding a ball. That way, we have more control over the dynamics of the situation and can determine the best course of action. Maksim has already betrayed us once and should be treated as highly dangerous and untrustworthy. He seeks to exploit our queen and gain power within our kingdom by force. Celestia won't be going through with this marriage, but she needs to ensure the safety of our people as she goes about finding a way out."

The council members exchanged weary glances, clearly unsettled by the risks they were taking.

"I'll do whatever I need to do to ensure our lands are protected from his grab for power—with the exception of marrying him."

"I'm sorry, Your Highness, but wouldn't marrying Maksim allow you to keep a closer eye on him and prevent him from being a larger threat?" Karina, who usually handled treasury matters, chimed in.

"I don't believe so. Maksim is volatile and aggressive. If I tried to control him, I'm of the firm belief that he would find a way to get me out of his way."

Karina seemed to understand her meaning, only nodding in response.

Leani stood from her seat at the long council table and began pacing in the middle of the room.

"What are Maksim's true motives? It's not as if he wants to marry you for love. He wants power. How can we give him the illusion of power without yielding part of our kingdom or risking the lives of any more merpeople?"

Celestia picked at her scales under the sleeves of her dress as she dredged through their past conversations for a possible solution.

"I still want to see him pay for what he's done."

"Of course, but perhaps that isn't an option right now. He has leverage, and we have nothing. We need time. We need him to back off before we can realistically do anything."

Celestia begrudgingly went along with plans for the immediate future. "Mesantia isn't doing well with their drought and subsequent shortages. What if we could promise him supplies while they restore their crops?"

Karina and Borris were speaking over one another at the suggestion. Apparently, they didn't have an abundance of food at the moment—unless they wanted to pull from the sea—and their coffers were healthy but not overflowing. They assured her it wasn't the best course of action.

They went around with suggestions and compromises, but they were no closer to a full-formed plan by the end of the hour. They agreed to call it a night, but to reconvene in the morning with actionable ideas.

It didn't settle Celestia's nerves, but it would have to do.

When she rounded the corner to her quarters, her heart nearly jumped into her throat with excitement when she saw Aura standing on the balcony watching the waves crash against the rocks.

She approached her on quiet feet and gently slid her arms around Aura's narrow waist, pulling her against her chest. Aura leaned into her embrace.

"How was the meeting?"

"Unproductive. But I'm confident we'll figure it out tomorrow."

Aura turned in her arms, her brow furrowed with worry. Celestia ran her finger down the crease, smoothing it away.

"Don't worry, it'll be okay. Trust me." A broad smile broke across her face. "Besides, I don't want to talk about that now. I want to show you something. Come with me."

She leaned her head out of the doorway, checking to her left and right before leading her out into the hallway and then the secret staircase to the right of her bedroom.

As she pushed through the discreet entrance, a whoosh of cold air blew back on them. Then they were temporarily consumed by the darkness. Within seconds, the bioluminescence came to life within their skin, casting a bright blue glow that lit their way.

They walked carefully down the seemingly endless staircase, the soft sound of water dripping on stone their constant companion. After what felt like an eternity, they reached the bottom, which opened into a large cavern. The waves lapped up onto the rim of the pooling water. With the face of the cave open to the sea, the ocean air blew cold and turbulent, and the white haze of the moon shone in, reflecting off the waves.

Celestia turned to Aura, seeing her face illuminated with joy as she took it in. The purple and green rock appeared alive with magic as the reflection of the colorful teeming waters bounced off the walls.

"Beautiful, isn't it?" she asked hesitantly, suddenly feeling self-conscious about revealing her favorite secret spot. Aura was a mermaid, after all; she'd likely seen her share of magical places.

Aura took tentative steps toward the edge, sinking to her knees to put her hand in the enchanted water. Upon contact, she tipped her head back and breathed deeply, her lavender waves blowing in the night breeze.

"Thank you, this is exactly what I needed."

Celestia couldn't help the proud smile that overtook her face as she approached the water's edge, sitting next to Aura.

"Do you want to go in?"

Aura nodded, reaching back to loosen her dress. Celestia intervened, helping her pull the corset loose before hesitating at the clasp around her neck.

"Go ahead," she urged in a hushed tone.

Celestia gently lifted the mermaid's long hair and moved it to the side of her neck, careful not to touch the delicate gills. She felt her breath finally escape when the fabric fell forward.

Celestia quickly unlaced her own dress before she could lose her nerve. Relieved of her clothes, she sat down on the edge of the cave floor's rocky edge, dipping her legs in. Bracing for the chill, she slowly sank herself into the water until it reached her collarbones.

"Come in?" Her eyes pleaded with Aura to say yes, to grant them this moment of serenity together. But she could see the fear lingering in her gaze.

"What's wrong?"

"I don't know how to swim without my tail." Aura nervously tucked a strand of hair behind her ear.

"Oh, right, sorry. That's okay, I'll show you." Celestia swam up to the edge, hands outstretched reassuringly.

Aura ducked her head shyly before slipping her own body into the water, frantically reaching her hands up onto Celestia's shoulders as she kicked her legs chaotically.

"It's okay. I'm going to hold your waist. Keep your hands on my shoulders." She pulled her closer, wrapping one hand firmly on each side of her hips to keep her afloat.

They were so close now that their noses touched. It was freeing, being like this, without any barriers between them.

Aura ran the back of her hand down Celestia's patch of scales reverently.

"Why do you always hide them?"

She stared at her scales, trying to see what the mermaid found so mesmerizing. With the light of the moon glinting off them, the mosaic of greens, blues, and purples looked like shards of gemstone. In that moment, she thought maybe they weren't so terrible after all. But still, she felt the need to be honest.

"People gawk at them. Their stares make me uncomfortable," she shrugged, trying to chase away the shame that started to creep in.

Aura bent her head low, a shy smile teasing her lips as she placed one soft kiss after the other down the rows of scales.

"Did you ever consider that they were looking at you in admiration? That maybe they were in awe of the magic within you?" She kissed her way back up and then leaned away, gently cupping Celestia's cheek. "I think they were, because I know I am."

Celestia took a deep breath before meeting her eyes. She couldn't help but be completely enamored by her. Her hair that reminded her of the sky before it released the rain, her skin that shimmered and sparkled like a thousand ancient stars, her lips that curved up in that way that always made her feel wanted, but, most of all, it was her pure heart that made Celestia want to cherish this woman for eternity.

When she shook herself from her thoughts, Aura was staring at her with the same awestruck expression.

The seconds passed as they watched one another, tentatively considering the strength of their bond and what it could allow them to overcome. The only sound was the whisper of the waves echoing within the cavern.

Celestia knew that Aura still had her doubts, but she also couldn't resist the pull between them now that she knew the truth of it. She believed with every fiber of her being that they belonged together, with or without magic.

With that certainty, she closed the small distance between them, pressing her lips to the mermaid's.

Their kiss was the clash of land and sea. Unruly as waves crashing upon the sand, washing away everything that came before.

Streams of water rose into the air around them, dancing and swirling, its movement reflecting the joy Celestia felt as their lips parted.

"Are you doing this?" She gazed down at Aura with wide eyes.

"No. Well, yes, but I think we both are."

Celestia's brow furrowed in confusion.

"The water is the source of our magic. Being submerged gives me access to my full power—and apparently the same goes for you."

Celestia's heart beat with new fervor as Aura's arms wrapped tighter around her and they watched the water shift and move in the air with their combined power at its strongest.

She resumed their kiss, trying to absorb all the affection she could from the mermaid. This simple moment of joy confirmed what she already knew. She wanted this, no matter how many obstacles they had to overcome. And if even if it didn't work, even if their souls were to be torn apart, it would be worth it. But if she had her way, she would have Aura. Now, tomorrow, forever. She could never let go of this feeling.

But then Aura pulled back. Her lips were red and swollen with the passion of their kiss, but her eyes were weary. The water slowly descended back into the waves of the pool.

"Celestia, we can't do this. I told you, this could never end well. You are of the land, and I am of the sea. What could we really have together? We're setting ourselves up for pain you can't even imagine."

"We are here together now, doesn't this count?"

"You dream of heartbreak? That we will have this great love, only for it to devastate us?"

Celestia grunted in frustration, pressing her forehead to Aura's. "Would it not be enough for you? To make the most of the time we do have, consequences be damned?"

Aura sighed, running her hand down Celestia's bare arms and resting them on her full hips.

The mermaid placed a kiss on her forehead before meeting her eyes. "No. I need all of you, forever. I cannot bear the thought of falling even more in love with you, only to live a life without you."

"That's why we have to fight for this."

"Meridia would never allow it," she said as if it were law.

"I don't care." Celestia felt a fire growing in her belly, fueling the words that pushed past her lips. "I am queen. I can make it so there's a life for us."

Her eyes were pleading, begging Aura to look past their current limitations and to the possibilities of the future.

"A human and a mermaid, that hasn't exactly worked before."

Celestia could feel Aura's body hardening against hers. She couldn't bear to let her pull away now.

"That was them, this is us. It's not the same, we aren't being forced to be together. We're meant to be together, you said it yourself. We have magic on our side. We can make this work, I promise."

Aura sighed against her lips, stirring something within Celestia that brought chills to the top of her skin.

"Trust me, please. Trust us." She nudged her nose against the mermaid's. Aura only nodded, but it was enough to release the breath Celestia held in her chest.

They spent the rest of the night lost in each other's company, enjoying the pull of the waves rocking their bodies peacefully as the moonlit sky watched over them.

There was no amount of time that would suffice for Celestia to take it in; she wanted to stay here forever. Instead, she committed as much as she could to memory, promising to hold onto this moment through the difficult times that lay ahead.

Chapter Twelve

Despite their late night, they woke early to practice Celestia's magic. She wanted to have a better handle on it before she met with the council. She knew they would want proof of what she was capable of before they agreed to any plans.

It seemed everyone had taken their task seriously, providing several logistically sound solutions to their Maksim problem.

In the end, they decided Karina's plan required the least risk. They had a vast amount of treasure stored in the castle that had amassed over generations, none of which was being put to any use. Karina suggested they trade it or have it melted down—a win-win for restoring their coffers and being able to pay off Maksim so he could afford to import the resources his kingdom required.

The problem was that he wasn't merely a concerned king. He was unpredictable and dangerous. He may refuse just to spite her. Celestia's powers were their backup plan for whatever went awry.

As the council members filed out of room, Celestia asked Leani to stay back.

"Did he accept the invitation?"

"He did. He should be here tonight."

As much as Celestia hated to admit it, he scared her. On her way to back to her suite she reminded herself that there was no time to panic; she had to present a brave face and move forward with the plan, no matter what. Everything was riding on her being the queen they needed.

Celestia entered her quarters to find assorted breakfast foods strewn across the floor and her balcony in disarray. Her hair stood on end as she took in the scene. When she left, Aura had been reading and enjoying a cup of Leani's tea.

She called for Aura, running to her room even though she knew it would be fruitless. She found her breath coming in short gasps as she frantically searched the empty rooms. When Aura didn't turn up, she knew she immediately needed to find Leani. She needed to question the guards and find out who took Aura, although she had a fairly good idea.

Celestia found her head of security at the gates reviewing protocol for when Maksim arrived.

"Leani, I need to speak with you urgently." She pulled her aside. "Aura has been taken."

"Are you sure she isn't just out?"

"Yes!" Celestia tried to reign in her panic. "It looks like there was a struggle, my balcony is a mess. She wouldn't have gone off. You know how nervous she is around humans."

Leani pulled her into a hug, clutching Celestia closely. Her stocky frame was comforting and warm as Celestia tightened her embrace for a moment longer. When she released her, she felt a bit calmer— at least enough to come up with a plan.

"We need to start a search. They can't have gotten far. We were only in the meeting for a little over an hour."

"That means someone was watching you closely."

Celestia ran her fingers through her thick, sea-foam-green hair in frustration. "It must have been someone working for Maksim, don't you think? He's going back on his word and making good on his threat. But why would he do it now, in broad daylight? It would've been much easier to steal her away when there were hundreds of guests around."

As they made their way back to the castle, Leani had every guard they passed looking for Aura.

"I think I know who's been helping Maksim." Leani stopped abruptly at the realization.

"Who?"

"Tolero."

"Why…" Celestia cursed at herself for not thinking of it first, kicking up sand. "You think he did this to get back at me?"

Leani nodded. "I do, but not just that. I think he's been working with him all along. The only question is what they plan to do now that they have her. They know that she's a weakness for you. They will exploit that."

Her mind was spinning with the revelation. Tolero and Maksim were working together. It seemed so obvious now. Tolero must have known that his time on Celestia's council was running short. They were always at each other's throats; of course he'd make another grab for power. It was fitting that he chose the most hostile kingdom to turn to.

He knew all their vulnerabilities, all of their defenses. Well, most of them that is. He wasn't aware of the extent of the magic she now possessed. But she wasn't confident he wouldn't try to torture information out of Aura. She hadn't been treated well the last time she'd landed in Maksim's grasp.

She needed to figure out where Aura was and how to get her back. Who knew how far he'd gotten with her?

The sense of urgency to find Aura was overwhelming when she parted from Leani and raced back to her room. They needed a plan of action quickly, since she would be expected at the ball soon. She needed to call her council.

She couldn't wander about the castle when they had hundreds of guests trickling in for the ball, so she had to ask Allora to find whichever council members she could grab quickly.

She soon returned with Leani, Karina, and Reedus. Celestia paced the floor as she explained the events that had unfolded and their suspicions. To her surprise, neither of the other council members doubted that Tolero would be capable of something like this.

In fact, she learned that it had been under Tolero's advisement that her mother had been forced to leave the ocean and marry her father. Apparently, he had a habit of using mermaids as political pawns. But she wouldn't allow Aura to be forced into a fate she didn't want. Her story wouldn't be a repetition of her mother's tragedy.

Finding that they were all on the same page about the problem at hand should have made it easier for them to agree on a course of action. However, Celestia was intent on going after Aura immediately, and the council disagreed.

"That may be part of their plan, to lure you away. That will leave us vulnerable," Reedus insisted.

"Perhaps he's right. Maksim will have dozens, if not over a hundred, of his own loyal subjects, council members, and guards within our walls. Who's to say what boldness he might turn to if you're not here to protect your people?" Leani shifted so she was standing directly in front of Celestia. "I'll go after her myself, with my most trusted guards. You know I'll do everything in my power to return her safely."

Celestia made eye contact with each council member and saw only genuine concern and careful consideration. For once, she felt she could fully trust those advising her. While she didn't like the idea of staying back and attending a ball, of all things, she understood the importance of her presence, especially considering this was supposed to be their engagement announcement. It all came together; why Tolero had been so pushy about the proposal, why he was so concerned when he had seen Celestia and Aura's growing affections, and why he'd revealed her secret at dinner.

All of this had unfolded right under her nose, and she'd been too wrapped up in her own world to see any of it for what it was. Perhaps Tolero had been right, maybe she had been an unfit ruler.

But not anymore. Tonight, she'd prove him wrong. She wouldn't let her people down, no matter the cost.

Chapter Thirteen

Once Leani and her council members departed, it was time for her to put on a full performance in front of hundreds of guests, and she intended to look the part.

She required help getting dressed for the ball. Her gown was much too heavy to manage on her own, not just because of the large, periwinkle skirt and long, silk train, but also the intricate beading that covered the arms and bodice. Fortunately, Allora and her assistant, Rayna, were able to attend to her.

First, they pulled her hair back, allowing the lower half to hang in loose waves, while the top half was twisted back at the sides. A special crown made of a ring of clear quartz was placed gently on her head. It was an engagement gift she didn't have the heart to deny, but she was intent on paying for it once everything was resolved.

As they prepared the gown, she admired the full skirt that opened in the middle, with a panel of sheer fabric that hugged her body. It was truly one of a kind. She only wished she could feel the same excitement about wearing it tonight as she had the first time she'd laid eyes on the custom gown.

Once it was unlaced, they helped her into the dress and her matching blue, satin slippers while she secured the lacy, silver masquerade mask. She slipped on her enchanted bracelet from Meridia, completing her look for the evening. She forced herself not to worry that they'd already used several beads training; she'd make do with what she had.

When she turned to look in the mirror, she gasped. It was truly the most beautiful garment she'd ever worn. The hundreds of crystals that ran across her arms and torso that proceeded to drip down the sheer fabric at the center of the skirt made her look like she'd just stepped out of the ocean. She even loved how the sheer fabric allowed for a glimpse of her scales between the crystal embellishments.

The fitted bodice complimented her figure quite nicely, accentuating her shapeliness and cascading around her gentle curves.

She allowed herself a few moments to soak in the vision of herself. While she might feel anything but poised and regal, she certainly looked the part. This dress would make the impression she intended—on her guests, her citizens, and, most importantly, Maksim. The message was clear: she was a queen, and she wouldn't be so easily coerced or intimidated. Cessadia was her home, and she was its protector, and he would be reminded of that.

The elegant music swallowed Celestia's steps and galloping heart as she approached the ballroom. She hesitated for a moment when she reached the doors, and then she gave the guards a nod to open them.

As the heavy, gold-inlaid doors swung open, Celestia couldn't help but gasp. She had forgotten that she'd planned an under-the-sea theme to make Aura's first ball special. While the fact that the mermaid wasn't here had tears threatening her eyes, she knew that she would've loved it.

Teal lights cast an oceanic glow across the walls and ceiling; even the movement of the lighting seemed to emulate being under the waves. When the lights caught the crystal-laden chandeliers, shimmers danced across every surface, reminding her of how the sun looked underwater.

She was almost lost in the moment, until she spotted Maksim's imposing figure in the crowd—even in the black mask, she would recognize him anywhere. As soon as their eyes met, he was closing in on her in long strides that ate up the distance between them much too quickly.

He swiftly planted a kiss on her cheek and pulled her arm into the crook of his elbow, anchoring her in place—as if she'd run off. "Hello, my beautiful betrothed," he said just loud enough for those around them to hear.

She forced her eyes to brighten and her features to turn up at his words, but she kept her voice quiet, so only he could hear. "I need to speak with you. Now."

"We must dance. Your guests have been patiently waiting for us to have our turn first. You wouldn't want to delay the festivities further, would you?" He didn't give her a chance to respond as he swept her dramatically onto the dance floor.

Maksim had always been a graceful dancer; it had been one of their favorite pastimes as children, dreaming of the days when they would host their own balls, with their own subjects, and ruling Cessadia together. Until he abandoned her, and then his father and older brother died of the same unidentifiable illness, allowing him to ascend his own throne—an interesting, if not suspicious turn of events.

Now, as they glided across the glimmering marble floor, she found herself so far from that fantasy that it was hard to imagine it had ever been a possibility in the first place. How could so much have changed that the boy who was her first love had turned into her greatest enemy? She supposed, in the end, it didn't matter. Across the years, that boy had lost his way.

She'd been doing her best to keep a joyous expression on her face, smiling and nodding at guests of honor she spotted in the crowd. But when he pulled her closer, she felt her mask slipping as her anger rose to the surface.

"Where is she?" she whispered below the music.

"Who are you referring to?"

"Aura," she hissed, his feigned ignorance dissolving her last ounce of patience.

"I'm sorry, I don't know anyone by that name."

"You know exactly who I'm referring to. Aura, the mermaid you released to me in exchange for my hand in marriage."

"Ah, yes. Forgive me. We aren't on as *intimate* terms as you are. Well, I was intent on keeping my word, until you went back on yours. I've been informed that you've developed a relationship with her and, even worse, never had any intention of upholding your end of the bargain."

"So, you don't deny it. You have her?"

"I do. And you won't be getting her back until we are married. Then, I'll decide what to do with her. Maybe I'll return her to the sea, maybe I'll hold her prisoner to keep you in line."

Before Celestia could respond, the song ended and one of the nobles cut in for a dance with her, which she couldn't refuse.

While she danced with several other guests, she ensured her gaze was carefully tracking Maksim. Their conversation wasn't over.

When she finally got a reprieve from dancing, her chest was rising and falling from exertion and a sheen of sweat sat heavy on her skin. Thankfully, the ocean breeze swept through the open sides of the castle. She made her way over to a balcony for a moment's rest. The temperature had dropped significantly, making the weight and warmth of the dress bearable.

As her gaze swept over the turbulent sea that lay before her, she couldn't help but wish that Aura had never been dragged into this whole mess, even if it meant never meeting her. She wouldn't be able to live with herself if any more harm befell the mermaid.

Her thoughts were interrupted by the comforting voice of an old friend. When she turned, Queen Violetta was standing before her. She was outfitted in a stunning gown with a fitted ivory bodice that flared at her narrow hips and slowly brightened into hues of greens, teals, and blues. It flawlessly complimented her dark brown complexion. She was a vision that captured the theme perfectly, reminding Celestia of looking out into the sea from the shoreline. The ensemble was completed with a metallic mask and shining teal and white pearls adorning intricate braids that brushed her lower back. And, of course, she was wearing her stunning crown that captured the essence of her realm—the base featured woven, golden stems and emerald leaves that flourished into lavender flowers and pointed amethysts. It was as elegant as she remembered.

She curtsied. While they were both royals, the queen was her senior and someone she had deeply respected since childhood.

Violetta bowed her head in response. "Queen Celestia. My how you have grown into your title. The last time you were in my kingdom, you were just coming of age."

The warmth and smile in her voice brought back pleasant memories of her last trip to the Lurrelean Forest with her father before he'd fallen ill. Violetta must have guessed where her mind had gone.

"I was sad to hear of your father's passing." She touched Celestia gently on the arm. "He was a great friend and ruler. I miss him dearly. But please know you are always welcome in my kingdom."

Celestia smiled at her kind words. "Thank you. It was lovely speaking with you, but I have something that I must attend to. I'll plan a visit soon."

With a bow of her head, she took off after Maksim as he exited the ballroom swiftly, likely taking the opportunity when she appeared distracted. She followed as discreetly as possible in the crystal-laden gown.

When he finally stopped, opening the door in front of him, she heard scuffling coming from the room. Before she could peek inside, he shut the door. She quietly approached, putting her ear firmly to the wood; luckily, Maksim was yelling.

"You were supposed to take her out of the castle as soon as Celestia arrived at the ball. Why are you still here?"

"There are too many guards. It's not as if she's easy to hide, look at her," Tolero hissed.

"Put her in a cloak and get her out of here. Every moment you stay here, the more likely we are to be caught. For this to work, we need the mermaid."

She needed to do something. With one deep breath, she pushed, sending the door flying open and revealing Maksim, Tolero, and Aura gaping at her. She immediately rushed to Aura's side, noting that she was wearing the same magic-suppressing chains she had the first time they met.

She pulled a bead from her wrist before anyone could stop her, casting a protective spell that erected a shield of water around Aura, repelling the men at her sides. It took them a moment to collect themselves. When they did, they were furious, but so was Celestia.

As Tolero pulled his dagger and Maksim approached her with violence in his eyes, she summoned her magic from where it slept. The glow that consumed her body from head to toe was so bright that it temporarily blinded the men, forcing them to avert their gazes as their eyes adjusted. Her skin was vibrating with the force of it; it felt like lightning bolts were striking through her limbs, but it wasn't painful. It was empowering.

She honed all that magic as she extracted another bead, holding it tightly in her palm and willing the water to comply with her intentions. While she'd been able to easily construct the bubble around Aura, it still surprised her when the violent wave tore from the bead as it exploded and swelled over the men, ready to descend upon them with all her fury.

The massive wave crashed to the ground with such force that it shattered everything in its path and swept the men into its current, dragging them out into the hall as they struggled and fought for breath from under the mass of water.

She hadn't thought her plan through, intending for the wave to remain in the room, and now innocent guests were at risk. In an effort to minimize the damage, she plucked another bead from the bracelet and a thick wall of water rushed vertically outside the doors of the ballroom, stopping the waves seconds before they crashed into the guards.

The two sources of water raged against one another. Her magic was keeping them at bay for now, but how long until it broke free and wreaked havoc on her guests? The foot of space that had been between the door and the wall of water was slowly closing, the waves pulsing forward. They needed to find a solution. Fast.

Chapter Fourteen

Celestia tried to focus as panic dug its claws into her mind. While she still had a few more beads, she didn't think more water was the right answer. Her power and control were waning. She could already feel herself starting to weaken from the sheer effort of holding the water at bay.

While she wrestled her brain for a solution, Maksim and Tolero were being slammed against the wall by the rushing current. It couldn't be comfortable, but as long as their heads remained above water, they'd live.

"Celestia, how did this happen?" The steady voice of Queen Violetta came from behind her.

"What are you doing out here? I thought everyone was in the

ballroom."

"They are, most of them. I was feeling nostalgic about our earlier conversation and went to visit your father's chambers."

"I can't hold this much longer. You need to get somewhere safe."

"I think I can help."

Before Celestia could respond, hundreds of large plants erupted from the ground, shooting up to the ceiling. Their stalks were at least a foot wide. Within a minute she could already see the water level lowering, the plants hungrily absorbing it. Celestia turned to Violetta, her mouth frozen in an "O".

Her father had told her that woodland magic was still powerful compared to the other kingdoms, but she hadn't expected that.

"It's only a temporary fix. But it'll do for a bit. We need someone more experienced with water magic."

That's when Celestia remembered Aura stuck in her orb of protection.

"I'll be right back."

Since she had to be the one to free her—what with it being her magic holding her—she had to trust that things would be fine until she returned.

"Guards, restrain those two and lock them in the throne room until I'm able to deal with them." She shot one last warning look at Tolero before she set off to get Aura.

When she returned to the room, Aura was still floating within the bubble, unable to do anything with the restraints nullifying her powers. A small smile spread across her worried face and her shoulders sagged with relief when Celestia stepped in the room.

She wasted no time, pressing her hands to the side of the bubble.

Slowly, water began to flow across the floor, emptying the orb and bringing Aura's feet safely back to the floor. Celestia immediately grabbed at the chains, trying to figure out how to unlock them.

"You need the key. Tolero had it last."

"We don't have time."

Celestia pulled one of the last few beads from the bracelet, imagining a controlled current within the lock, forcing the mechanism to turn. She wasn't confident that it would work, but moments later the restraints dropped from Aura's wrists.

The moment they sprang free, Aura wrapped her arms around Celestia's neck, embracing her like she thought she was never going to see her again. If there weren't a crisis on their hands, Celestia would have leaned into that hug for as long as possible. However, they only had so long until the plants succumbed to the exorbitant amount of water they were currently housing.

"We need to go. I need your help with something. I don't know what to do with all of the water I conjured and it's only a matter of time before it takes down the doors." Celestia ran a frustrated hand over her face. "Why wouldn't Meridia think of this?"

Aura winced. "I hate to defend her, but we don't use this magic on land. It's likely she didn't anticipate it."

Celestia only sighed, accepting that as a real possibility, and made her way back out into the hall. When they rounded the corner, Aura gasped.

"It took all of that to contain the water?"

"Yes. Was there not supposed to be that much?"

"I didn't expect it, what with you just learning how to control your magic. But I suppose since you're of royal blood, it makes sense that your powers would be stronger than most once you learned to wield them. It's lucky you were able to contain it with these for a few minutes." She moved her hair off her shoulders, raising her hands. "No matter, we can do this together."

Celestia looked at her questioningly, mimicking her stance.

"Are there any clear exits, free of people?"

Celestia's mind began to race under the pressure. She reminded herself to breathe, running through all the rooms and passages on this floor and below. And then she remembered the hidden staircase that opened into the one that came off her floor.

"There's a stairwell at the end of this hall to the right. Can we really move all this water?"

Aura nodded. "Have someone prop it open for us, then we can send the water down that way and into the cavern. It'll flow back into the ocean from there."

Overhearing them, Violetta was already on her way over there. Once she was finished, they resumed their stance, ready to take control of the water. With their collective efforts, they were able to summon it out of the plants and slowly guide it down the stairs. By the time they were done, they were both sweating and panting heavily.

Aura slumped with relief when the last of it trickled past the doorway.

Celestia bowed deeply as Violetta approached. "Thank you. I couldn't have done it without you. I owe you a great debt."

The queen squeezed Celestia's arm. "Friends do not owe friends debts." She smiled. "Perhaps a favor if I'm ever in need."

Celestia returned the smile. "Of course. You can always count on me."

Once they said their goodbyes, Celestia joined Aura on the floor, not even caring that it was wet.

"What now?" Aura's voice was barely above a whisper.

"Now, you go rest. I'll deal with them."

"No. I want to come."

It was the most force she'd ever heard Aura speak with, so she wasn't going to deny her. She deserved to be there.

They gave themselves a few minutes to catch their breath, but, once they pulled themselves together, they were anxious to get to the throne room.

"One minute, I just need to ensure the guests are tended to and gather the council. You stay here." She directed Aura to a seat and then made her way back into the ballroom to make arrangements. When she nearly plummeted to the floor, she reminded herself to ensure someone dried everything before the guests departed so no one was injured.

Before entering the throne room where the traitors waited, Celestia grabbed Aura's hand. She needed the reassurance that she wasn't going to be taken from her again. Although, with her magic restored, she wasn't sure they'd even get the chance to attempt it.

The door creaked ominously as they entered together, her council in tow. The guards had restrained Tolero and Maksim, their arms chained behind their backs. The men greeted her with matching scowls.

Celestia didn't bother taking her throne this time. She didn't expect to spend much time deliberating. There was no doubt in anyone's mind that they were guilty.

She let go of Aura's hand to clasp her own in front of her, strolling around the table.

"You two are traitors to this kingdom. Especially you, Tolero. My father—and my father's father, for that matter—trusted you. We believed you had the best intentions for our people, *all* of our people, at heart. Clearly, we were wrong." She stopped in front of them. "How long have you been scheming behind my back?"

He turned his face away, dismissing her demands for information.

She slammed her hands on the table, forcing him to whip his head back in her direction. "How long have you been a traitor to your people?"

That got a rise out of him.

"I've never betrayed *my* people, only you have."

"I have fought for what's best for everyone in Cessadia. Why do you resent the merpeople so much? You were the one who helped orchestrate this entire union."

He scoffed. "That was when I thought they'd empower us, not be a drain on our resources and alliances."

Celestia noticed Aura's jaw clench from the corner of her eye.

"Of course, why would I expect anything better from you."

Aura stepped forward. "And what of the murdered princess? Was that you as well?"

Tolero turned slowly in her direction, a vicious sneer showing his disdain. "What does it matter who killed her? She's gone, and we're in chains."

"Because it does." Aura began to glow with her power, the bioluminescence casting an azure light over everyone. "Tell me of your own free will, or I will force the truth from you. Your choice."

Tolero only stared at her, his brows furrowed in disbelief. When he did not speak of his own volition, Aura shrugged and closed her eyes. When she opened them again, her usually lovely eyes were now a milky white, as were Tolero's.

"Tell me who killed Princess Estrellia," her voice echoed throughout the chamber, taking on a haunting quality.

Tolero's lips pressed together in a thin line, but, after a moment of quivering, he was forced to speak against his will.

"I did and I don't regret it. It was a worthwhile risk to try to bring these two kingdoms together. Having Maksim take his place as king could have pushed Cessadia into a new era, one where we weren't forced to consider the merpeople in every decision. One where our people, and those of Mesantia could flourish. But then you took hold of our Queen, derailing all of my carefully laid plans."

The churning colors slowly returned to Aura's eyes and Tolero's were once again a nearly-obsidian brown. They only stared at one another for a moment.

Aura's voice was hushed when she finally spoke. "That's how you did it. That's how you took my tail. You used Estrellia's heart to harness her magic and use it against me." A single tear escaped her unwavering gaze, trickling down her cheek. It was tragically beautiful as it shimmered against the iridescence of her skin.

Celestia forced herself to remain in place when all she wanted to do was wipe it away.

"Tolero, I, Queen Celestia Valtimeri, hereby charge you with the murder of Princess Estrellia. You will face trial and heed Meridia's decision regarding your fate."

She turned to Maksim.

"King Maksim of Mesantia, you will be tried for conspiracy. You should make arrangements for another to take your place. I'll be calling the Council of Kingdoms to strip you of your title and rights to your lands."

"You can't do that!" he spat.

"I can and I will. With the rulers of Odressean behind me, you'll be done for. You should have never betrayed me, Tolero. Whatever fate befalls you is only your burden to bear."

Chapter Fifteen

With Tolero and Maksim's capture, they learned what they needed to return Aura's tail. This was it, their last day together, and it was rapidly coming to a close.

Celestia stood on her balcony, overwhelmed with the conflicting emotions of relief that they would finally be getting justice, happiness for Aura's freedom, and the impending heartbreak she was going to face when she returned home.

She wondered if Aura was disappointed that she wouldn't be here to see Maksim brought to justice. At least with Tolero she could watch from the waters. Her heart clenched at the thought of seeing her again.

She didn't hear the mermaid approach, of course, but she could feel her presence, the energy of their bond buzzing between them as she stepped through the entryway and out onto the balcony with her. Aura gently put her hand over Celestia's, urging her to turn and face her.

She searched the mermaid's glowing eyes. There were already tears welling there. The sight alone broke all of Celestia's promises to herself not to cry.

"Is it time?"

Aura only nodded, gently wiping tears away with her thumbs that pressed warmth back into her wind-chilled cheeks.

Celestia lost all ability to speak as the mermaid turned, pulling her behind with their interlinked hands. She didn't notice a single person as they walked down the cascading steps, through the castle, and, finally, onto the sand. Her mind was reeling with all the reasons she couldn't and wouldn't ask the mermaid to stay.

Only when the cold evening air brushed her face did she snap back into the moment. But still, she stood frozen until she could summon the courage to take the next step forward. Every foot they closed between them and the sea was bringing her closer to the end of everything. Unbidden, the tears returned, blurring the landscape in front of her until she could no longer tell how far they had to go. When the cold water lapped across her toes, she choked out a sob.

She was no longer the restrained queen she had always strived to be. She was a broken woman losing the one thing she treasured most. Her world was crumbling before her like the sand beneath her feet.

Aura was standing with her back to Celestia, her lavender hair drifting in the breeze, revealing delicate shoulders that were shuddering with silent sobs.

Celestia held her mouth closed tightly, refusing to allow the words she wanted to scream to escape. She wouldn't hold Aura prisoner here like her mother had been. She deserved a better fate. She deserved her freedom.

They only had a few minutes until sunset, the rays quickly disappearing into the horizon. Their time was nearly up. As soon as the sun set, and the moon began to rise, Aura would have her tail again and have to return to the ocean.

Aura's desperate words broke through the crushing silence. "I love you. I know it's only been a few weeks, but I do. And I know it's right that fate drew us together, even if the loss of you will be an undying ache that haunts me for the rest of my days."

Celestia only shook her head, unable to speak.

Aura pressed delicate kisses on each of her cheeks, chasing away the tears now pouring down her face. "I'll never stop loving you."

"Knowing that isn't enough."

"It has to be." Aura kissed her so intensely it stole whatever was left of Celestia's resolve. "I love you, don't forget that. I'll always remember you, Celestia. But I don't want you to torture yourself by waiting for me to come back. This is goodbye. There will be another who can love you the way you deserve, someone who is meant to exist in your realm. Let them."

Before Celestia could form a response in her grief-riddled mind, Aura slipped out of her arms, moving quickly into the water until she was waist high. She never would have known the mermaid had turned if she hadn't watched her tail flick the surface as she dove beneath the water.

The moment the last glimpse of pink and lilac scales disappeared beneath the waves, whatever strength she had left within her evaporated. Celestia sank to the sand, watching the moon rise hopelessly. She knew she should get up and return to the castle, but she couldn't leave. Instead, she sat there well into the freezing night, hugging her knees to her chest as she stared emptily out into the dark abyss of the open sea.

She woke suddenly, the sharp ocean air and bright sun greeting her. She'd spent the entire night on the beach. Memories came flooding back to her. It was the culmination of her worst nightmare, but she knew it was only harsh reality. She forced herself into a vertical position, finally noticing that she wasn't alone.

Meridia was watching her from a few feet away.

Celestia stood abruptly, brushing the thick sand from her body and face. They stared at one another for several moments, only the breaking waves disrupting the eerie silence of the empty beach.

"You let her go." Meridia's tone was flat, but her brows were raised in surprise.

"Of course, I love her. I would never ask her to sacrifice her home."

"For some, love is possessiveness. Many with your power wouldn't simply let the one they love out of their life, no matter the cost." She eyed Celestia suspiciously.

"That's not true love then."

She grunted in agreement.

"Why are you here?"

"I may have misjudged you. Perhaps I've been too harsh on

you by assuming you were of the same make as your father and his forebears."

She appeared deep in thought, so Celestia remained silent, confused as to where the merqueen was going with this conversation.

Within Meridia's hand appeared a necklace with the same beads as the bracelet. She extended it to Celestia.

"I'm sorry things have been so strained between us, Celestia. Perhaps, we can try to start anew. I think it's time you're trusted with the power that was meant to be yours."

Shock rocked through Celestia, stealing her voice, so she only nodded.

Meridia opened her mouth, then closed it again, thinking better about whatever it was she had planned to say. "See you tomorrow, Celestia." And with that, ending their unexpected conversation, the merqueen was gone.

Chapter Sixteen

$\mathcal{C}$elestia forced herself through the motions as she and her council made their way to the beach for the sentencing two days later. Two days after Aura left with her heart, and she had devolved into emptiness. Time passed without her noticing. The only thing keeping her from completely falling apart was her duty to get justice for Estrellia, for Aura, for all of Cessadia. So here she was, being the queen they all needed.

Even still, she couldn't help her wandering gaze that desperately searched for any sign of the mermaid watching from the water. There was none. And she shouldn't have been surprised. Aura said she wouldn't return.

Celestia waited at the edge of the water since she and Meridia couldn't stand side-by-side. Her council and the rest of the crowd were there to bear witness. The wind ripped through the air violently, mirroring the mood of the merqueen. It had been a volatile few days convincing the other rulers to converge for the Council of Kingdoms and preparing for the sentencing. Tension hung thick in the air as they awaited the verdict.

Meridia's grave voice broke the silence. "Tolero Postera, you have committed the vilest crime against one of our kind: murder. Do you deny it?"

Tolero remained silent, refusing to acknowledge the merqueen.

"Your silence confirms your guilt then." Her voice was deep and ominous. "Do you know what we do to those who kill a mermaid?"

This captured Tolero's attention, his head swiveling slowly toward her, but, still, he didn't speak.

"Drowning. And not the quick kind."

When she smiled, Celestia could have sworn she saw the gleam of long fangs extending from the corner of her mouth, but she didn't dare to let her gaze linger.

His eyes went wide with alarm. "Celestia, Your Highness, surely you're not going to allow this?" he begged. There was not a note of the usual haughtiness in his voice, only the desperation of a man not prepared for death.

The thought of murder for murder didn't sit well with Celestia, but this wasn't her punishment to dictate, and she respected their ways enough to stay out of it. Tolero had already sealed his fate.

"Your punishment is Meridia's decision. I won't interfere. You knew enough about mermaid law to foresee the potential consequences of your actions. As I said before, you have no one to blame but yourself, Tolero."

The guards stepped forward, dragging him as he kicked up sand and shouted obscenities. When he passed Celestia, he spat at her feet.

"Stop," she gritted out to the guards, who then swiveled toward her.

She reached up, pulling the blade from the center of her trident, and slashed it down the side of Tolero's face, watching as the blood he couldn't wipe away dripped into his eye.

"Let this be a reminder. Anyone who dares to harm one of my own will pay the consequences. And if you disrespect your queen, you will be repaid two-fold." She let her gaze linger over every person in attendance before turning back to the guards. "Take him."

Two ancient-looking mermaids rose eerily from the depths, smiles matching Meridia's as they peeled him away from his escorts and drew him under water. The splashing and screaming turning to silence within seconds.

Meridia turned her attention to Celestia. "I expect you'll ensure Maksim pays for his transgressions?"

Celestia only nodded, looking to the other royals who did the same.

"Very well." And with that, Meridia was gone, no ceremony or departing words. She was satisfied with her vengeance.

The Council of Kingdoms headed directly to the throne room, deliberating for hours about what the best course of action would be for both punishing Maksim and nullifying the threat Mesantia could potentially pose, depending on who took the throne in his place.

Celestia rubbed a hand across her brow. "I hate to say this, but I truly think that Tolero was the orchestrator behind all of this. He must've been the one to retrieve the spell, he was the one who poisoned Estrellia and stuck the blade into her chest, and he was the one leaking our secrets."

"What's your point?" King Sordin, who ruled over the Turrulean Valley, asked.

"I think that Maksim should be stripped of his title and punished, but I don't think it should be nearly as severe as the sentence that was passed for Tolero."

Murmurs of agreement passed around the table.

"What do you propose?" Queen Violetta inquired, curiosity crossing her features as she leaned forward.

"I think it would be best to exile him from the continent and replace him with a regent of our mutual choosing. That way, we can protect all of our interests and ensure that he has no influence here again."

"All he's known his whole life is Odressean. You would banish him from the entire land?" Queen Aradya of the Scorian Desert questioned.

"I would. None of our crowns or our people are safe while he's plotting for more power."

Aradya assessed her carefully, but then nodded, seeing the reason in her proposal. "So, he's exiled then. We can reconvene in two months' time. I think, for now, we should allow his natural successor the opportunity to prove himself worthy of the throne."

They all agreed, not wanting to interfere with one another's affairs unless necessary.

"One more thing." Celestia stepped toward Maksim. "There's a chance he might be able to sneak back in if someone doesn't recognize him. I can't allow it."

"What do you propose?" King Sordin asked.

"I want to mark him, so that everyone knows what he is." Her eyes hardened as they moved over Maksim, who was sitting chained to the table in the corner. She swept her gaze over the others, looking for any objections.

There were none, so she leaned down and pressed the tip of her trident to his forehead. When she removed it, the distinct symbol of Cessadia glowed in the center. "If he ever tries to land on these shores or anywhere in Odressean again, it will come to the surface, branding him a traitor."

"Ingenious. It's incredible what can be done when one has full access to their magic," King Sordin murmured wistfully. "It's done then. Meeting adjourned."

Afterwards, Celestia found her feet moving in the direction of the beach, so she followed them. When she reached the shoreline, Meridia was waiting there. It made sense now that she'd called her or, more specifically, compelled her to come here.

Celestia took a deep breath, wondering what Meridia could need now.

The merqueen waited for her to take a few steps into the water before she began speaking. "The other night, I found Aura lingering just off the shore, watching you sleep. She barely kept enough of herself submerged to sustain her life. She was that desperate to be close to you, if only one last time." Meridia swam a few feet closer. "I have never seen such a connection between one of our kind and one of yours. Although, I suppose, you aren't so human after all."

Celestia unknowingly had wandered thigh-deep into the water, wanting to catch every word.

"Aura told me she bonded to you, that you're her soulmate." Her gazed lingered thoughtfully on Celestia's. "What if I told you I could grant Aura the gift of living between land and sea?"

"I would say it's her choice."

Meridia's lips twitched, something that could have been a smile if she had allowed it. "She said the same thing when I offered her this deal."

"What deal?" Celestia's brow slammed down in suspicion. She had been caught off guard by Meridia's odd behavior, but now everything seemed to be aligning.

"In exchange for Aura's freedom to come and go from the ocean and her mermaid form as she pleases, you would need to agree to an unbreakable bond to protect the merpeople until the end of your natural life, allowing no further harm to come to us."

"I've already agreed to protect you."

"This is no simple agreement, girl. This is a blood oath bound by your magic—yours and Aura's. Should harm befall us, you will be stripped of your magic, and she of that which allows her to transition back and forth."

"I won't make this decision without her. I want to hear directly from her that this is what she wants. Then, I will agree to your terms." She crossed her arms over her chest.

Meridia swept her fingers across the top of the water and, moments later, Aura emerged, glistening with droplets that sparkled against her skin in the sun.

Celestia struggled to force the words out against the lump in her throat. "Is this what you want?"

"Yes." There wasn't even a second of hesitation.

"Won't you miss it? Your home?"

"You're my home." She swam closer, running the back of her hand down the side of Celestia's face. "You're not trapping me. This is my choice. Now, agree to her terms and let me come home."

Celestia nodded. "I accept the deal. How do we seal it?"

"Each of you must sacrifice a piece of your magic." Before Celestia could ask the question on her lips, Meridia explained, "Those scales on your arms, I need one."

Celestia's brow furrowed, unsure how that was possible. An ancient knife formed within Meridia's palm as she grabbed her arm.

"Hold still, this will hurt more than you think." She pressed the knife against her skin, the power within it hot, searing her skin as she removed a single scale.

Celestia gritted through the pain that forced tears from her eyes and caused blood to spring from the lip she was biting into.

Next was Aura. She leaned back so the lower portion of her tail was peeking up through the water. Meridia braced her hand, then repeated the process. Aura's eyes squinted in pain, her usual soft smiled turned to a grimace. Celestia imagined the salt water stung the open wound as she tucked her tail beneath the waves again.

Her jaw dropped open as Meridia ingested both scales, her nose wrinkling in disgust.

Meridia laughed at her sardonically. "Celestia, you truly have been sheltered from the old ways. Hopefully, Aura will give you the education I should have. It's time you knew your mother's people, if only to better protect us."

Suddenly, Aura clenched her hands around Celestia's forearms as she doubled over gasping in pain.

"What's wrong? Aura, are you okay?" When she didn't answer, worry built within her. But another moment later, she straightened, standing on two legs.

"Will it always hurt like that?"

"Yes. A small price to pay, don't you think?"

"Yes, of course."

"Good. I'll be seeing you, then." Without another word, the merqueen disappeared into the ocean once more.

Celestia began walking back toward the shore, their hands interlinked. As they made their way back to the castle, Celestia felt like she could breathe deeply for the first time in ages.

They'd fallen into a deep sleep, both exhausted from their time apart, but when Celestia woke, Aura was nowhere to be found. That familiar panic momentarily seized her, but she reminded herself they were safe now.

After a quick search, she found the door to the staircase had been left open. Celestia followed the winding stairs down into the depths below the castle.

The salty air was thick down here, and the evening breeze sent a chill across her skin as she stepped out into the opening.

There Aura sat, her legs dipped into the illuminated water, her gaze set far away.

"Homesick already?" Guilt pulled at Celestia's empty stomach.

She patted the stone slab. "I already told you, you're my home. But I do crave the comfort of the waves. I'm glad I have this." She gestured her hand around the space.

Celestia slipped her legs into the water, joining the mermaid.

Aura twisted her torso so they were facing one another. "So, what now?"

Celestia watched her features carefully, searching for any sign of regret or longing. There was none. All she could see was pure contentment. It was all the confirmation she needed.

"Marry me?"

The mermaid held her breath, searching Celestia's eyes desperately. For what, she didn't know—maybe the same things she was.

"I told you, if you dared to dream with me, we could have it all. So, will you marry me? Let us live out whatever years we have left happily?"

The smile that broke across the mermaid's soft features was brighter than the burn of a shooting star as she leaned in, resting her forehead against Celestia's.

"Yes." The words were a whisper that tickled her lips in a way that set her soul and skin on fire. "I am yours, there is no magic or man strong enough to come between us."

Chapter Seventeen

The next few days were busy with preparations. The kingdom was buzzing with excitement, both for a new era of peace and at having a magical being as their queen.

While the citizens of Cessadia had long lived amongst the merpeople, they never intermingled. They remained on land—except for the parts of the coastline designated for human use—and, for the most part, the mermaids remained in the underwater city.

Aura had finally started to let her guard down a bit. She walked throughout the castle freely, laughed more frequently, and even accompanied Leani into the city to get fitted for a dress. Once she was introduced to the wonders of the streets of Cessadia, she prolonged her time out in public.

There was nothing that would have made Celestia happier, except for the impending wedding day.

Guests had started to arrive from all over the continent, including the kings and queens of surrounding realms, as well as friends Celestia had made during her visits. During the feast the night before the wedding, the castle walls were brimming with people, filled to capacity with light and joy.

With Maksim and Tolero out of the picture, everyone seemed more than happy to preserve the amicable relations they'd established long ago. Of course, Maksim's successor wasn't in attendance, but that was to be expected.

For now, they would enjoy their new beginning. The evening before the wedding passed in cheers, dancing, and good company. They couldn't have asked for more.

Celestia stood at the end of the long walkway, which was adorned with stunning, lavender-and-white flower arrangements. She could see Aura at the other end of the identical walkway that led to the altar. She found herself wanting to sprint down the aisle, but she stood patiently, waiting for the music to begin.

In the moments she had left, she fussed with her strapless silk dress, making sure the flowing fabric lay smoothly against her figure, and the silver stars and moons lined up just right along the slit that opened up to her left hip. Meanwhile, Allora arranged the sheer cape she wore that was inlaid with intricate silver detailing that sparkled under the slowly setting sun.

Finally, the music started, a sweet romantic melody that signaled for them to start walking. She was frozen as Aura came closer into view. That was until Allora pressed her hand firmly on the center of her back, giving her the courage to put her body in motion, her feet closed the space eagerly. With every step she took toward Aura, her stunning gown appeared in more vivid detail. It was perfectly her.

The billowing sleeves hung open, the fabric meeting in the middle at her wrists, elbows, and shoulders. The bodice was corseted and adorned with intricate pearls and shells. The lower portion of her dress was a delicate tulle, allowing for a glimpse of her glittering skin to shine through. Her long, lavender hair was studded with pearl barrettes and carefully pulled back, soft waves framing her face.

When they finally made it to the altar, Celestia allowed herself to breathe again. Aura was quick to grab her hands as they stood before Leani who proudly served as their officiant. Celestia floated through their vows, which they wrapped up enthusiastically.

"To daring to dream."

"To forever."

When their lips met, the world fell away, and they were swept away into pure bliss. As Celestia opened her eyes, she noticed they were both glowing so brightly, the guests in the first few rows were squinting against the light.

Slowly, the glow receded and the guests stood, clapping and cheering. They were celebrating with a fervor that surprised her, bringing tears of joy to her eyes.

There was one last part of the ceremony. Aura needed to be crowned. Celestia had labored over the crown's design with the royal jeweler over the last few days, but the final result was nothing short of perfection. It was delicate and elegant just like her. And when it was presented to her, the mermaid's mouth popped open in a pleased "O," and Celestia knew this was the perfect start to their new reign.

She lifted the crown, which was comprised of mostly hand-selected shells along with tastefully intermingling pearls, pink sapphires, and, of course, moonstones to match those captivating eyes. With it in place, Celestia embraced her wife, her queen, and guided her back down the aisle passing the throngs of her people, *their* people, who congratulated them all the way back to the castle.

When they entered the palace, music was swelling throughout, echoing from the open ballroom and into the marbled halls.

As soon as they entered the ballroom, Celestia encircled Aura in her arms and they drifted across the dance floor. Others joined them, creating a sea of swaying bodies that moved in unison to the music.

The final rays of the sun caught on the dozens of chandeliers that lined the ceilings, casting rainbows throughout the room. The only thing that rivaled its beauty was Aura's wide smile as she relaxed into Celestia's arms.

When they had done their queenly duties of greeting and thanking all their guests, Celestia led Aura back out of the castle, leaving their shoes at the edge of the sand as she trudged determinedly toward the slowly shifting water. It was peaceful tonight.

"What are we doing out here? It's freezing."

"It's a surprise."

Celestia finally stopped when the water hit her ankles, removing her gown and tossing it on a rock, high out of the waves' reach.

Aura stood there watching her with her mouth agape in wonder.

Celestia continued moving forward. The pain hit her all at once, causing a gasp to escape her lips. Aura lurched forward in fear, but she put her hand up, letting her know she was okay. Once the cramping abated, she dipped below the waves, emerging where the water was shallow enough for her to display her gold and blue tail.

Aura brought her hands to her face. "What is this? Is this real?"

"It is. This is your wedding gift. Meridia approved. Now that the kingdom is a place of peace, I'm taking a few weeks off to spend with you. You're going to show me your home."

"What if something changes?"

"I trust Leani and my council to take care of things while I'm gone. As for the mermaids, Meridia and I worked together to establish a spell that would protect the shoreline." She waved her in.

The mermaid swam out into the water, transforming into her natural state. She flung her arms around Celestia, planting a kiss on her lips will such fervor that it nearly forced her below the surface.

The thought made her panic for a moment, but then she realized that it wouldn't matter, she could breathe underwater now. She pulled Aura below, grabbing the sides of her face and deepening their kiss.

In this moment, with her magic singing through her veins, the water holding her in a gentle embrace, and Aura's lips anchoring her in place, Celestia realized she truly had everything she ever wanted. Someone who loved her. A oneness with the sea. And the freedom to lead as she'd always dreamed.

Acknowledgements

To my mom,

Thank you for reading and re-reading—okay, and re-reading—this story to help me get it right. This was my very first book baby and I couldn't have done it without you. I'll always be grateful for your support.

To everyone who contributed to this book,

Thank you for helping to make this book possible. I truly value every individual who puts work into making my stories the best that they can be.

To my readers,

Thank you for reading my work. I hope this book brought a little light into your day and that Celestia showed you that even fat girls can be beautiful queens and get their happily ever after.

To everyone who read this story in Curves & Magic first,

Having you support that project means the world to me! Thank you for taking the time to read my story when I was just getting started on my author journey and helping me support a cause I care deeply for. I hope that we'll see many more plus size main characters in the future.

About the Author

Alexis C. Maness is a mood author with a special place in her heart for dark stories. In her books, you can look forward to reading about plus-size and morally grey main characters who'll make you swoon and maybe even root for them against your better judgment.

When she isn't glued to her keyboard weaving words into something worth reading, you'll most likely find her with a glass of sparkling wine in hand, falling in love with the villain of her latest dark romance read. She lives in San Diego with her bossy yet adorable cat, Satine, whose dedication to sitting in one spot for a long time is the main reason these stories have finally made it to you.

Keep up with Alexis' latest releases on her socials:
https://www.tiktok.com/@authoralexiscmaness
https://www.instagram.com/authoralexiscmaness/

Sign up for her newsletter to get sneak peeks and updates first!

Made in the USA
Middletown, DE
09 June 2023

32187088R00080